Death By Theft

A Josiah Reynolds Mystery
Book Nineteen

Abigail Keam

Worker Bee Press

Copyright © 2023 Abigail Keam
Print Edition

ALL RIGHTS RESERVED

No part of this book may be reproduced or transmitted in any form without written permission of the author.

The history is true, but the rest is fiction.
The book is not about you or your friends,
so don't go around town bragging about it.

Book cover by Cricket Press.
Author's photograph by Peter Keam.

Special thanks to Melanie Murphy and Liz Hobson.

ISBN 979 8 863824 42 0
101523

Published in the USA by

Worker Bee Press
P.O. Box 485
Nicholasville, KY 40340

Books By Abigail Keam

The Josiah Reynolds Mysteries
Death By A HoneyBee I
Death By Drowning II
Death By Bridle III
Death By Bourbon IV
Death By Lotto V
Death By Chocolate VI
Death By Haunting VII
Death By Derby VIII
Death By Design IX
Death By Malice X
Death By Drama XI
Death By Stalking XII
Death By Deceit XIII
Death By Magic XIV
Death By Shock XV
Death By Chance XVI
Death By Poison XVII
Death By Greed XVIII
Death By Theft XIX
Death By Betrayal XX

The Mona Moon Mystery Series
Murder Under A Blue Moon I
Murder Under A Blood Moon II
Murder Under A Bad Moon III
Murder Under A Silver Moon IV
Murder Under A Wolf Moon V
Murder Under A Black Moon VI
Murder Under A Full Moon VII
Murder Under A New Moon VIII
Murder Under A British Moon IX
Murder Under A Bridal Moon X
Murder Under A Western Moon XI
Murder Under A Honey Moon XII

1

I climbed the ladder placed under the Pin Oak tree and very carefully cut the branch holding the bee swarm—must have been over seven thousand honeybees huddled together in a ball protecting their queen. I scrambled down the ladder holding the branch with the clinging bees, but you know I'm not good at these things since my accident. Slowly I made it to the ground without falling off the ladder or dropping the branch. With my right hand, I swiped the clump of bees causing a huge mass of bees to fall into my swarm box. I shook the branch and thousands of remaining bees flew up around me and then settled on the white sheet placed under the swarm box. The honeybees marched like little soldiers into the swarm box bottom opening, each eager to be near their queen and gobble the honey I had smeared on some of the frames.

Happy that the bees were cooperating, I put the top of the swarm box back on and watched the bees go into the bottom entrance. Within an hour, all the bees would be in the box setting up housekeeping. Only then would I move the swarm box to a hive where I would install frames thick with the bees and a queen. For three days, I would keep them locked up, so to speak, in the hive before I removed grass clippings blocking the hive entrance and let them do their bee thing. At that time, I would open the top of the hive, look for the queen or signs that she was laying eggs. If I found no sign of baby bees, I would remove a frame from another hive which had a queen cell.

Happy with the successful swarm catch, I left the swarm box alone and retreated to my golf cart when my cell phone rang.

I answered, "Hello?"

"I thought you were coming to see the colt?" Shaneika Mary Todd asked.

Shaneika was my criminal lawyer. If you have to ask why I might need a criminal lawyer, then you haven't lived in these parts for long. I'm famous for stumbling over dead bodies. It's a curse.

"I was. I mean I am—but came across a swarm. Let me finish up here and I'll be over."

"Don't tarry too long. The stable employees will be letting the horses out to the pastures soon."

I looked at the swarm box. The bees were hurrying inside. "Shouldn't be too much longer. I'll be there as soon as I can."

"I'll be in the breeding barn. Comanche has a cover this morning."

"Okay. I will meet you there as soon as I can," I replied, hanging up. I watched bees march into the swarm box and figured they would be okay. I would pick the box up later. I got in my golf cart and petted Baby, who had been waiting patiently. "I'll get the box after we see the new colt. Don't let me forget my bees, Baby."

My two hundred pound English Mastiff sneezed and put his massive paw on my shoulder.

"Good boy," I said, removing his paw and scratching him behind the ear. I started the cart and headed over to my next door neighbor's farm to find Shaneika and visit the colt.

The farm was owned by Lady Elsmere. She and Shaneika had bred their horses, Jean Harlow and Comanche, to produce a colt which they hoped would win the Kentucky Derby. It was Lady Elsmere's dream to win the Kentucky Derby before she died. The colt had been born a few weeks back, but Shaneika banned visitors as Jean Harlow was a skittish mother. The fact that Shaneika had invited me today meant Jean Harlow had finally calmed down.

I really wanted to see the colt and wished Lady Elsmere and Shaneika well on their path to racing glory in the Kentucky Derby, but I had grown disenchanted with horse racing. Too many accidents on the racecourse.

Yeah, I know. I'm a hypocrite. I make money

boarding race horses. I catch the overflow of pregnant Thoroughbreds whose offspring are trained on Lady Elsmere's farm. I don't take in stallions anymore as they are too difficult and high-strung. It's a nice income but whenever I can catch a racing official's ear, I bring him to task about racing horses too young and the need for the Thoroughbreds' added protections. My advice goes in one ear and out the other. Oh, well, I do what I can.

I hear the horse owners have meetings about increasing the safety in the racing industry, but there are still too many spills on the racing course. That's why I don't go to Keeneland Race Course during the racing season.

Baby and I reached the breeding barn and waited for Shaneika. I texted her that I was outside. I don't like to witness live covers. I find horses' breeding encounters to be noisy, violent, and traumatic. The mare has to be covered in protective gear as the stallion can easily harm her with his sharp hooves and teeth. I always feel sorry for the mare.

I looked up from my phone and glimpsed a groom leading Comanche to a pasture. He must be done for the day.

Shaneika came out and waved.

"How did it go?" I asked.

"Very well."

"You're breeding Comanche too much. He can't

catch his breath. The dew is still on the grass, and you've got him covering a mare."

"I need the money, Josiah."

"Too much breeding weakens a stallion."

Shaneika rolled her eyes. "That's an old wives' tale."

"Maybe. Maybe not."

"Before you berate me more, let's visit the colt." Shaneika's hazel eyes brightened. "He's a beauty. Black with a white star on his forehead and four white stocking feet."

"You want Baby along?"

"He visits the nursery barn on a daily basis. The mares are not bothered at all by him and even Last Chance likes to play with him."

"How does a colt play with a Mastiff?"

"Last Chance prances around Baby and tosses his head. Baby licks him. Sometimes they share a treat."

It was always a mystery to me who my dog visited during the day while I worked in the bee yard.

"How's Jean Harlow doing?"

"Much better. For a few moments, we thought Jean Harlow might reject her baby, but she came around. I'm not sure Lady Elsmere will breed her again though—as a dam, she is far too nervous."

I muttered, "I see. The horse had postpartum depression."

Shaneika gave me a playful slap before putting Baby in the back of the golf cart. "Let's go. I need to get back to my office for my first appointment."

I pushed on the pedals, and we moseyed over to the nursery. Excited, I entered the barn with Shaneika leading the way. It was still very early, and the mares were with their offspring in their stalls, quietly munching on hay. They would be let out when the grass had dried. However, kicking and neighing erupted from one stall.

Shaneika shot me a worried look. "That's Jean Harlow. I know her cry."

We both rushed to the stall. "What's wrong?" I asked, seeing Shaneika's alarmed facial expression.

Shaneika swung open the stall door and pushed a nervous Jean Harlow out of the way.

I grabbed the mare's halter and led her out into the barn aisle. She was jumpy and hard to handle, so I shouted for aid. "Can someone help us, please?"

Shaneika ran out of the stall and began checking the others frantically.

"What is wrong?" I asked again, handing Jean Harlow over to a nursery groom who led the horse back into her stall.

Shaneika screamed, "WHAT'S WRONG? WHAT'S WRONG? LAST CHANCE IS MISSING. THAT'S WHAT'S WRONG!"

2

I doubled-checked the stalls and followed Shaneika outside. We searched around the barn and found an aged white Toyota with Juan Gomez sitting inside. He was the night watchman for three barns. If anyone knew what had happened to the colt, it would be him.

"Juan! Juan!" Shaneika called, running to the car.

Baby ran ahead to the car and jumped up, placing his paws on the open window ledge.

I followed and saw Shaneika push Baby out of the way.

"Juan, what has happened to Last Chance?" Shaneika asked frantically.

The man didn't answer but looked asleep. How could he sleeping with all this racket?

"Juan, answer us! Juan?" I said, tapping on the windshield.

The man didn't respond, so I opened the car door.

Juan toppled over and spilled out of the car, stiff and gray in pallor.

Shaneika and I both screamed and then froze, not quite understanding what we were witnessing. Baby reacted first, sniffing Juan and pawing the man with his massive paws.

"Stop that, Baby," I commanded. Coming to my senses, I leaned over and felt for a pulse. Looking up with dread, I exclaimed, "He's dead, Shaneika. Juan is dead!"

3

Within twenty-five minutes Lady Elsmere's farm was swarming with cops. Shaneika and I were told to wait in Lady Elsmere's house, which we call the Big House—a white, antebellum brick mansion complete with front and back porticos, massive columns, and balconies.

We waited in the kitchen with Lady Elsmere's chef—Bess. She put cinnamon coffee cake and steaming cups of coffee before us.

I nibbled at mine—I was never one to turn my nose up at Bess' coffee cake, even when upset.

Shaneika jumped up from the table. "I can't just sit here. I'm going to look for my colt."

"The popo told us to wait here," I warned. I had my share of troubles with the police, and if Shaneika was in the slammer too, who was going to get me out?

"I've got to look for the colt. They are investigating a murder. My horse is not high on their agenda. Please, Josiah," Shaneika pleaded.

What could I do?

I said, "Bess, can you hang around the phone until we get back? If we get arrested, we'll need someone to post bail for us." I was referring to the landline, as Lady Elsmere did not allow smart phones in her home since one of her *friends* had surreptitiously snapped inside pictures of the Big House and sold them to a well-known magazine. Even her staff is required to ask for guests' phones before they are permitted inside the house now.

Bess stopped mixing the bowl of cake batter and put down her wooden stirring spoon, handed down through generations of Dupuy women. "What shall I tell the police if they come looking for you?"

Shaneika and I glanced at each other. We didn't want to have Bess lie to the police, so Shaneika said, "Tell them we had to step out."

I followed Shaneika out the side door and through the pastures, my bee yard, and onto my gravel road. I said, "Go through my stable to double-back and take one of Lady Elsmere's cars to check the roads. I'm going to inspect the back pastures and the river. Meet you back at the Big House."

"Okay. See you later."

I checked my sheds first. No sign of any disturbance and no colt. Then I checked the pastures—my Scottish Highland cattle, Rove goats, baby llama and mama, peacocks, two rescue racehorses, various sheep, rescue donkeys, and boarded horses including my own horse—Morning Glory. I went over and held out an apple. Morning Glory plodded over and took the apple from my hand. "Have you seen a little black foal with a white star on his forehead?" I asked.

Glory neighed, wanting another apple. I happened to have another one in my pocket and held it out for her. "Good girl. Good girl." I petted her muzzle and scratched her behind the ears before I made my way to the Butterfly—my mid-century home on the cliffs of the Palisades.

Before I tell you more of this story, let me introduce myself and explain what the Butterfly is. My name is Josiah Reynolds, and I'm a beekeeper living in the Kentucky Bluegrass—horse country. I make my living from selling honey at a local farmers' market. I also board horses and own a catering business. I rent out my home, the Butterfly, for events. The Butterfly is built from local timber, slate, and limestone. The entire back wall is glass so one can see for miles. It's perched on the edge of the Palisades which is a cliff system bordering the Kentucky River. There are no steps in the Butterfly and it has extra wide hallways. I call it a cradle-to-the-grave house as it can accommodate an elderly person's mobility needs quite handily until death.

It was from this cliff that a rogue cop pushed me, and ever since, I have a bad left leg and need to wear a hearing aid. I shattered my teeth, fractured my jaw, and broke so many bones that I lost count. I should have died, but instead of falling one hundred feet to the river below, I landed on a ledge forty feet down hitting tree branches all the way. I made my way back to the land of the living after a long convalescence.

Before the accident, my husband left me for another woman and had a love child with her. That wasn't the worst of it. He stole my share of our assets, my good jewelry and designer dresses, which he gave to his girlfriend. I managed to keep the farm, but lost my job as an art history professor on track to becoming the next dean in my department at a local university, due to the scandal and gossip. I should have sued.

I refused to give my husband a divorce until he returned my possessions including my money, but he up and died, taking the secret of our assets with him. I know he gave everything to his mistress. I just can't prove it. I was on the edge of bankruptcy for several years, but fought my way back to solvency. I have money in the bank now and have doubled the size of my farm. I still deal with physical pain, which gets less every year, but now my kidneys are threatening to shut down. The less said about that the better.

The only odd thing is that after I recovered from my fall, I seem to stumble over dead bodies all the time. Poor Juan, the watchman, makes nineteen so far. I'm beginning to think I'm a jinx.

Don't you dare agree with me. It was just a thought out loud.

Arriving at the Butterfly, Baby and I jumped into my VW van as my golf cart had been impounded by the police. I slowly drove down the rutted gravel road to the river with my windows down. Every so often I would stop the van and see if I could hear a whinny. Nothing except for song birds calling to each other.

I got to the river dock where Lady Elsmere and I keep our boats and was greeted by two cops looking for evidence. They looked up at my van in surprise and gave orders to exit.

BUSTED!

Now my van was impounded, and Baby and I were escorted by a young policeman back to the Big House. We both were basically shoved through the back kitchen door by the cop who stood guard outside. To make matters worse, Detective Drake sat at the kitchen table eating cinnamon coffee cake. Bess poured him a large glass of milk and gave me a wide-eyed stare behind him. The stare pleaded with me not to antagonize the good detective.

Detective Drake didn't like me, but he respected my particular gift—solving puzzles. While chomping on coffee cake, he gave me the stink-eye. "I thought my officers told you to stay at the Big House until we could get your statement."

"I have given my statement twice."

"You haven't given it to me," Detective Drake said, wiping his mouth with a linen napkin.

"What would you like to know?"

"For starters, what were you doing at the boat dock?"

I answered, "Looking for Jean Harlow's colt."

"You think a young colt swam across the Kentucky River?"

"I think whoever shot Juan could have smuggled the colt down the river."

"What makes you think Juan Gomez was shot?"

"Uh, maybe because of the hole in the back of his head."

"Did you know he had been shot when you opened the car door?"

I looked at the cup of coffee Bess placed before me. The smell of the coffee and the talk of head wounds made me feel queasy. I grabbed my stomach while answering Drake's question—"No, we didn't know until he fell out of the car. When we tried to help, we noticed the wound then."

"Both you and Miss Todd."

"Yes."

"Did you both touch the body?"

"I know I did. You'll have to ask Miss Todd. I don't remember if she touched the man or not."

Drake gave me a concerned look. "You look rather pale, Mrs. Reynolds. Surely seeing another dead man shouldn't upset you. You've had so much experience with corpses."

I made a face. "Very funny, Drake. Get on with your questions."

"Did you notice anything else that might help the police?"

I shook my head.

"What did you do after discovering the dead Juan Gomez?"

"Called the police. What do you think we did?"

"Did you continue looking for the colt?"

"Shaneika, I mean Miss Todd did, but I stayed with the body."

"Did you go through the man's pockets or his car?"

"No, of course not," I lied. You better believe I took pictures with my phone.

"So we won't find any hair fibers of yours in the car?"

"You might on the body." What was Drake up to asking me all these questions? Surely he didn't think I had anything to do with Juan's death! Did he?

"We noticed Mr. Gomez's key ring beside the car. Did you touch it?"

"I don't remember any key ring or keys for that matter. Must have fallen out of his pocket when Mr. Gomez fell to the ground."

Drake asked, "You think the lost colt and the murder of Juan Gomez are connected?"

"Of course, I do! Don't you?"

"At the moment, there is no evidence to connect the two crimes."

"Oh, for God's sake! Juan was the night guard for the nursery barn. He was shot during the kidnapping of the colt because he was a witness, or by someone trying to take his gun during the crime. It seems as plain as the nose on your face that the two crimes are connected." I sat down fuming.

"Did you disturb anything?"

"Again, Miss Todd and I touched the body to see if Juan was alive. That's all." Did Drake sense I was lying? Gosh, I hope he didn't ask for my phone.

Drake mused, "I'm surprised no one heard the shot."

Bess said, "There are three guards on duty each night. There are big fans inside the barns. If they were checking inside the barns, they might not have heard."

"I see cameras everywhere. How can I get the footage?"

Bess cut another piece of coffee cake for Detective Drake. "You'll have to ask my father about the security measures. I'm not privy to all the security protocols."

Bess's father is Charles Dupuy, a direct descendant of Aaron and Charlotte Dupuy. Aaron was Henry Clay's slave from boyhood. He saw Charlotte on another plantation in Kentucky and asked Clay to buy her, which Clay did. Aaron and Charlotte were married and travelled to DC when Clay became Secretary of State. Charlotte sued for her freedom there in 1829, twenty-eight years before the Dred Scott decision. She was one of the first enslaved females who sued for the right to be free. Unfortunately, she lost her case and was sent to the Deep South as punishment. Henry Clay's family finally gave freedom to Charlotte, Aaron, and their children, Charles and Mary Ann. Or maybe the Civil War did. It's not clear.

So you see Charles Dupuy, who managed Lady Elsmere's estate, came from a gutsy heritage. Since Lady Elsmere had no heirs, and Charles has served her faithfully for years, she is leaving him everything if she dies from natural causes. I pride myself in playing a part in the inheritance. I thought the Dupuy family deserved a piece of the money pie. I'm also the one who had Lady Elsmere put in the will a clause about dying of natural causes. I adore the Dupuy family, but where there are millions of dollars at stake...one never knows what people will do.

I butted in. "Look, we all know this was an inside job. The culprits had the codes to the gates, knew where the colt was located, and made off without a hitch. Because they brought a gun means they knew there were security guards and expected a confrontation."

"You previously told one of my officers that Juan was sitting in the driver's seat."

"That's right."

"Were there any signs of a struggle?"

I replied, "Not that I could deduce."

"There was a half-wrapped candy bar beside him. I think Juan was going to eat his candy as a pick-me-up and someone came from behind and shot him."

I replied, "For what purpose? They could have tied him up or bumped him on his noggin."

"Did Juan carry a gun?"

I shrugged. "It was mostly to kill copperheads."

"There was no sign of a struggle and in all likelihood Juan never saw his assailant. So ladies, the question I am asking is—was the attack personal or did it have to do with the theft of the colt?"

Bess looked worried. "This is just terrible. Juan has worked for Lady Elsmere for over eight years. He was a good employee. Always on time."

"What do you know about his personal life, Miss Bess?" I asked.

"He had three grandchildren which he would bring to see the horses. He only worked part-time. He was easing into full retirement. This is such a shame. Lady Elsmere is torn up about it."

Detective Drake gave me a hard look for butting in and then asked, "Married?"

"Yes, but they are separated. They haven't lived together for quite a while."

"What's her name?"

"Valeria Gomez. She lives in the Cardinal Valley subdivision. That's all I know."

"I need to have his employee records. Things of that nature."

"Again, ask my dad. I never touch his things."

Detective Drake asked for another piece of cake.

Bess looked at her watch. It was nearly noon now. "I'll make you a nice sandwich as well. You must be hungry."

"I didn't have breakfast," Drake confessed.

"May I have a sandwich, too?" I gave a sad look at Bess.

Baby went over to Bess and whined, a common tactic he used to get fresh water and treats. I supposed he picked that up from me.

Glad to have something to do, Bess worked quickly to make sandwiches and fetch Baby some water. It was then her father, Charles, entered the kitchen. Taking off his muddy boots, he carefully laid them on a mat by the door and put on slippers that he used in the house as not to scuff up the polished floors.

Detective Drake looked with interest at the boots. "Why are your boots muddy?"

Charles sat across from the detective and his daughter immediately put a cup of steaming coffee in front of him. "We have two ponds on the farm. We were dragging them to see if someone killed the colt and threw him into a pond."

"One of my officers with you?"

"Several. Your men are still at the ponds," Charles reassured.

"Dad, you got any ideas?" Bess asked.

"It is my opinion this was a professional hit with inside help. I came back to get a list of employees for the police."

I asked, "Any suspicions, Charles?"

"We'll see who shows up for work today, or more important, who doesn't show up."

Drake demanded, "I'll need everyone's phone numbers and addresses."

"Of course, Detective. I'll do it right now." Charles grabbed his coffee and went into his office, which was located off the kitchen. A minute later, we could hear the printer. When it stopped, Charles came out and handed several sheets to Drake, who looked surprised at the number of people who worked for Lady Elsmere.

"The list contains accountants, financial advisors, close friends who had access to the farm, etc," Charles explained.

Drake gave me a knowing glance as I also had access to the farm's security codes.

I held up my hands. "I had nothing to do with this. I am a clean slate."

"It's just funny that wherever you are, people are found deceased. Wasn't it just last Halloween you found a dead man in Lady Elsmere's corn maze?"

"I do believe I solved the case for you."

The detective harrumphed.

Amelia entered the kitchen. She was Bess' sister and a companion to Lady Elsmere who saw to the old woman's needs. Amelia gestured to Drake. "Lady Elsmere will see you now, Detective. Please keep it brief as she is very distressed."

Drake nodded and followed Amelia into the library where Lady Elsmere waited.

I rested my chin on my fist and lingered as I didn't really know what to do. I was completely stumped.

Mike Connor, Lady Elsmere's horse trainer, and Shaneika trudged into the kitchen.

I looked at Shaneika who looked positively drained. "Well?"

"We checked every barn and pasture down to the river and then the major horse farms along the road."

"Nothing," Mike added. "I've got some feelers out but everyone's being quiet. This is quite some mess." He rubbed his hand through his thick hair.

"There hasn't been horse rustling in the Bluegrass since the 1970s," I remarked. "How is Jean Harlow doing?"

Shaneika said, "I'm going to see about her now. I've put in a call to Velvet Maddox."

Velvet was the local horse whisperer and water witch. She was a fierce little sprite of a woman who, on more than one occasion, warned me of danger. She's always right, so I listen to her with serious intent.

"That's a start," I replied. I had never seen Shaneika as distraught as her lower lip quivered.

Mike, noticing it too, put his arm around her. "We'll find him. Don't worry."

"Last Chance is my future. I've got everything riding on him," Shaneika said.

Out of the corner of my eye, I saw Detective Drake walk out to his car. He must have left via the library patio doors. I smiled as Drake looked like he was dragging his tail between his legs. So Lady Elsmere had given Drake his comeuppance. There is a god after all.

Amelia came into the kitchen again. "Josiah, she wants to see you."

Shaneika started forward, but Amelia put up her hand. "Just Josiah, Miss Shaneika."

I gave Shaneika a beseeching glance before following Amelia. "Come, Baby." My dog padded after me as we trailed Amelia to the library. She opened the door and bade us to enter before quietly closing the door after us.

"June?" I said. June was Lady Elsmere's first name, which was used in private. In fact, she was June Webster from Monkey's Eyebrow, Kentucky. Her first husband had invented a doohickey that made them rich, but he died in Europe when they were on tour. She then met Lord Elsmere, who liked the homespun Kentuckian a great deal. He made a pact with her. He would make her a great lady if she would marry him, but not ask about his personal life. You get my drift.

Intrigued, June acquiesced, and the two had many wonderful years together before Lord Elsmere passed away. She came back home to Kentucky and bought the horse farm next to the Butterfly. Brannon, my husband, restored her antebellum home, and the three of us became great friends. I call her Lady Elsmere in public as does everyone else, but June in private.

She was sitting by the fire with a blanket wrapped around her legs. I had never seen June look so frail. She wore no makeup, none of her usual dragon red lipstick, and none of her fabulous jewels. Her eyes looked rheumy and her hands shook slightly.

"June, why do you have a fire? It's warm outside."

"Is it? It feels cold."

Baby went up to June and placed his head on her lap, looking up at her as he whimpered. It was Baby's way of comforting.

June caressed his soft fur as she stared into the fire.

I sat opposite her. "June, I'm so sorry. I know how much that colt meant to you."

"Josiah, I want you to do something for me. The police will poke around looking for my horse and they may find the person or persons responsible for killing Juan, but I need results fast. I need muscle and someone whose hands are not tied by niceties of the law." June looked at me with those watery blue eyes. "Call her, Josiah. Call her. I need Asa."

4

I went home. I must tell you that my heart was beating fast. Of course, I would do as June asked, but I worried about it. My daughter was a loose cannon. I never knew where she was on any given day. It could be months before I would hear from her. Asa was supposedly an art insurance investigator, but I knew she was into darker, more dangerous work. I don't know if she was a private contractor who worked for the CIA or any one of those nefarious organizations.

Asa had toiled for the Secret Service but was drummed out when she spoke out about the lax conduct of the other agents, who drank and chased women when on travel assignments. For bringing to light a dangerous situation that might have compromised the President's life, her male superiors punished Asa until she had enough and resigned.

I worried about my daughter. I wanted Asa to settle down and have a family—a normal life that did not include chasing bad guys about the world. Yet, it was the life she had chosen, and I had to accept it, although begrudgingly.

Baby and I returned to the Butterfly. I gave my English Mastiff some fresh water and poured myself two fingers of neat bourbon. After sipping my drink and taking a deep breath, I sank into my teal Florence Knoll mid-century sofa and pulled the old fashioned landline phone onto my lap. I lifted the receiver and dialed the number Asa had given me for an answering service.

A woman on the other end answered. "Yes?"

I exhaled and uttered, "Rosebud."

Then I hung up.

5

Asa had stashed herself away at a mom-and-pop motel in Key Largo recovering from a bullet wound. It was a 1950s motel that owner, Eva Hanover, had renovated keeping its mid-century allure and Florida charm while installing all the conveniences of a more modern age. Even the furniture was chic and modern, which relaxed Asa as it reminded her of the Butterfly, her mother's home.

Hearing her phone beep, Asa casually glanced at it. The number 99 popped up. Asa stared at it for a moment and then jumped into action. She called an associate in Lexington, Kentucky who had been hired to keep tabs on Josiah.

A woman answered.

"It's me."

"I've been expecting your call."

"What's happened?" Asa asked, dreading news that her mother might be seriously injured for she loved her mother more than anyone in the world.

The woman quickly told Asa about the stolen colt and the night watchman who had been murdered.

Asa asked, "Any suspects?"

"The police are coming up blank."

"I see. Assemble the team. I'll be in Lexington within four hours." Asa hung up and then dialed for a helicopter to take her to the Miami airport. From there, she would charter a private plane home. She was still healing from a bullet wound and broken ribs from a previous assignment and was not in peak condition to tackle another mission, but home was calling. She had to go, so she swallowed some pain pills and packed a light bag.

Asa hurried to the front office where she called out for Eva, the proprietor. Eva came out of the back office to the front desk. "Yes?" she said warily as she never knew what to expect from this dark-clad woman with dark hair and wary eyes.

Asa slapped three thousand dollars on the desk. "I have to go away. Keep my bungalow for me. No one needs to go inside."

"Doesn't it need to be cleaned?" Eva asked, staring wide-eyed at the bundles of fifties.

Asa shot back, "No."

Eva asked, "When will you return?"

Not responding, Asa turned and strode out of the office. A black sedan awaited outside the office to take her to the helicopter pad. She settled into the back while a man in the passenger's seat handed her a dossier about the incident involving Juan's murder: the police report and photos of the crime scene including the stall of the missing colt. "I trust no one can detect that you hacked into the Lexington Police Department's computer."

"In and out within minutes. No one can follow the trail," the man responded, looking smug and telling the driver to put the pedal to the metal.

"I want a complete background check on this murder victim, Juan Gomez."

"You got it, Boss."

"Any theories?"

The hacker replied, "Shaneika Mary Todd has made lots of enemies because of her legal work, but then so has Lady Elsmere over the years, although this could be a simple case of jealousy. Maybe someone thinks the colt might have a chance of becoming a Triple Crown winner and doesn't want it to happen?"

"What about my mother?"

"Other than discovering the body with Shaneika Mary Todd, your mother doesn't seem to be involved."

Asa ruminated, "That won't last long. She will stick her nose in this case just like she always does, but I'm gonna beat her to the punch."

The hacker smirked. "Good luck with that."

Asa leaned back and pondered on how to keep her mother out of harm's way. She was worried. Something in her gut told Asa this was not a simple case of horse stealing. Something darker was afoot, and Asa fretted over her mother's involvement, especially since she secretly knew of her mother's declining health. Even if Josiah's health was perfect, sooner or later, her mother would meet her match one day and falter. There were only so many times one could cheat death.

And the specter of death was something Asa knew all too well.

6

I didn't know Asa was already in town—the little twerp.

No one knew at the time.

Lady Elsmere rang me several hours after I made the call. "Anything?"

"Not so much as a peep. Sorry, June."

"Do you think she knows we need her?"

"She does, I'm sure. Asa is either overseas or can't help us. I'm sorry." I could feel Lady Elsmere's desperation over the phone and didn't know what else to say.

Asa was always a wild card. My daughter was different, even as a child. She always had a rigid sense of right and wrong. There were no areas of grey—just black and white when it came to morality.

Asa never forgave Brannon when he accused her of causing his business to falter when she testified before Congress about Secret Service agents drinking and whoring on oversea assignments. After Brannon left me for his mistress, we found out he stole my share of our assets, and he had sold his portion of the architectural firm to his partners months before. Asa had nothing to do with his business problems. He just made the accusation up. Yeah, both were heavy blows. I guess we each felt we were walking on hot coals with him.

When Brannon deserted us, Asa never spoke to her father again, even though he pleaded with her. If he called, Asa would hang up on him, not saying a word, just putting the receiver back on the hook. When he tried to see her, she would just turn and walk the other way.

At first I was happy Asa was so supportive of me, but as time went on, I realized that I was being petty, and she should have a relationship with her father. I knew Brannon loved her, and our troubles with each other had nothing to do with our daughter. Nothing I said would dissuade Asa from the cold treatment of her father. Brannon died without Asa ever acknowledging him.

I resigned from my teaching position at UK because of the gossip when it came out that Brannon had left me for a woman who was Asa's age, and the two had a love child. It was impossible to teach students who snickered in class. What's more, I realized my chances of becoming chair of the department had gone out the window.

I knew from an early age that Asa was different

from other little girls. She never wanted to play with the dolls I bought for her. Instead, she wanted toy guns. Then Asa wanted real guns. I put the nix on that, but it gave me pause.

I read up on autism, psychopathy, sociopathy, and other disorders. Asa would fit some of the profiles, but not the more dangerous attributes. She loved animals, was popular in school, a straight A student, good at sports, and was on the student council. Asa excelled at everything she tried. I was so very proud of her, but there was a side to Asa which seemed off—a cold, collected side she kept hidden from others, including me.

Asa had a steady boyfriend whom I thought she would eventually marry, but when high school ended, she went off to college, ending the relationship. That boy became my pal Detective Kelly, and he was devastated. It took him years to get over the hurt. "Why didn't Asa say goodbye?" he would ask. "I thought she loved me."

I had no answers for my good friend, Kelly, for I knew Asa had loved him. Asa's behavior confused me as well, and I always wondered when it would be my turn for the cold shoulder. Since I hadn't heard from her, I was terrified that time had come.

I could have just wrung my not-so-sweet daughter's neck when I discovered Asa had flown to Kentucky immediately after my call.

7

Asa had gone to a safe house she had purchased years ago. It was a little unassuming farm house, which sat far from the road. A dismantled lawnmower sat in the driveway with tools situated on a tarp close by and perennial flower baskets hanging from the porch looking as though someone lived there year round.

Someone would go once a week, tidy up the yard, water the flowers, and collect the mail. Neighbors believed a recluse by the name of Mr. Snidely lived there. That was the name on the house title and on the mailbox, but Mr. Snidely never existed.

Asa posed as the man's niece, and if any of the neighbors stumbled upon Asa, she would say she was taking care of his house as he was either in the hospital or on a trip with friends. No one thought to question Asa why they had never seen Mr. Snidely.

She spent hours in a secured room with a satellite-connected computer where she researched recent horse sales, tracked down rumors, and read articles about the horse theft. She had agents watching the Nashville, St Louis, Bloomington, Memphis, Louisville, Cincinnati, and Lexington airports. If someone was trying to smuggle that foal out of the state, she would know about it. She had other operatives searching all the horse sales, even non-Thoroughbred transfers. Last Chance could be passed off as another breed. Finding nothing untoward, Asa decided that an on-the-ground human approach was needed. Computer searches could only get her so far. Now was the time for old-fashioned gumshoe intelligence work.

Discarding her usual black garments, Asa softened her appearance by donning jeans, knee-high tan leather boots, peach blouse, tan corduroy jacket, and a paisley Hermes silk scarf. The next morning she got up at five and travelled to Keeneland Race Course to have breakfast at the Track Kitchen. She moseyed around the tables presumably getting cream for her coffee or ketchup for the hashbrowns while surreptitiously listening to people's conversations. Asa thought it odd no one was yakking about the missing colt as horse rustling should be on the lips of all the trainers, jockeys, grooms, and racing fanatics. She was sure gamblers were already betting on the horse's reappearance and the culprit's identity. Hearing nothing of use at the Track Kitchen, Asa went to the training track to mingle among other horse enthusiasts watching the horses work out.

She leaned on the railing next to Short Nose Joe, a gambler of some note, a track bum, and a former jockey. He folded his racing form in half and put it in his jacket pocket and kept his gaze on the track. Speaking in a low voice, Joe said, "I was wondering when you were going to show up, Asa."

"You know why I'm here."

"Sure do. Jean Harlow's foal is still missing." He picked a piece of lint from his shoulder. "The old woman know you're here?"

"No."

"It's gonna be hard to keep that from her." Short Nose Joe pulled a cigar out of his shirt pocket and lit it.

"What can you tell me, Joe?"

"Word is the colt was stolen for revenge."

"Revenge for what?"

"That I don't know."

Asa asked, "Is the colt still alive?"

"Don't know that either."

"Every barn and shed in a hundred mile radius has been checked. Is the colt still in the state?"

"Like I said, I don't know if the colt is dead or alive, but you know the Bluegrass sits on a bed of limestone. Lots of caves. A wise gal might learn something by lookin' underground. Just saying."

"Is that what you've heard, Joe?"

"Just saying."

"Who can tell me for sure? The colt needs his

mother. He's not weaned."

Joe made a slight nod with his head. "Dandy Dan might know. Of course, he's not talking but if it's dirty, he'll know about it."

"Where is he?"

"He'll be here when the Off Track Betting windows open."

"Do you think he'll talk to me?"

"I know you two go way back but no. I figure he'll give you the bum's rush, but then what do I know," Short Nose Joe said, pulling on his cigar.

"Always a pleasure, Joe," Asa said, slipping some bills into the man's pocket as she passed.

Joe turned to watch the horses while pulling out his racing form. He would keep his ears open for Asa, but thought she was treading into dangerous territory. Surely she must know this was the work of a syndicate. And if that was true, then Asa's life wasn't worth spit.

It would only be a matter of time before Asa was found dead as a warning to others.

8

Asa entered the off track betting room at Keeneland, looking for Dandy Dan. He was sitting by himself in a corner wearing a crisp, white monogrammed shirt, designer jeans, and a pair of Christian Louboutin loafers without socks. Freshly shaved and immaculately groomed down to his manicured nails, Dandy Dan was a professional gambler who knew every sleaze in town. His side gig was information. She knew if there were rumors about Last Chance, Dan would have heard them.

"Hello, Dan."

Dandy Dan didn't even look up from his racing form. "Hello, Asa. This is a surprise."

"You don't seem surprised."

"I saw you enter." He motioned for her to sit down. "What brings you to town?"

Asa sat down in a leather chair beside him. "Let's cut the crap, Dan. You know why I'm here."

"Ah, the colt. Poor little thing."

"Ah, yes, the colt. Where is he, Dan?"

"How would I know?"

"Because you know what's going on in this town. I need that colt returned to his mother. Now, where is he?"

"I don't know, but even if I did, I wouldn't tell you. I value my life."

"So that means it was a professional job."

"I don't know who did it." He returned to his racing form, ignoring Asa.

Asa was in a great deal of pain and wanted this interview over, so she leaned over, digging her nail in the back of Dan's hand. "You've got a problem with me if you don't squeal." She didn't have the patience to play twenty questions with Dan. She needed another pain pill as the last one was wearing off.

Dan tried to pull his hand away but couldn't. "Stop it, Asa! You're harming me."

Asa let go. "You're gonna find out if that colt is still alive and where he is."

"And if I don't?"

"Then you'll have me to worry about. You know how I can be, Dan. Don't force my hand."

"You were always too much of a thrill junky, Asa. Even in college, there was too much of an edge to you."

"You didn't seem to mind when I saved you from being beaten up by those drunken frat boys."

"I remember. You did save my butt. I was grateful. Am grateful."

"I got word that it might be a local job due to revenge. Revenge on Shaneika Todd or the old woman?" Asa reached for Dan's hand again.

He pulled his hand away and put it in his jean's pocket. "Stop it. You're making a scene, and I don't like pain."

"Then spill."

"Word is it was done because they want Lady Elsmere to stop pushing. It was a warning."

"A warning for what?"

"To stop pushing for reform. She's been after state and national legislatures for more humane treatment for horses in the racing industry."

"Tell me more," Asa urged.

"The old gal wants a law that horses have to wait until they're three years old to start racing. Pushing the age limit back would make the Kentucky Derby horses four years old instead of three because they have to be stakes winners first in order to qualify."

Asa wasn't surprised. Most evil in the world had to do with money. "Seabiscuit was five years old when he won against Triple Crown winner War Admiral by four lengths in 1938. Older horses can achieve wonderful things."

Dan replied, "Four is when Thoroughbreds retire and start breeding, making real money for their owners.

Money is not in the racing. It's in the breeding. Racing is only to make a name for the horse and for the glory. Trophies, large purses, and ribbons impress the deep pockets who want to invest in the next sure winner. Most owners in the business figure four is too old for racing. They want Lady Elsmere to shut up and quit making a fuss."

"Dan, we all know that Thoroughbreds are physically too young to race at two. There are just too many spills and broken bones on the track."

"I don't disagree. I'm just telling you the conventional wisdom."

"Who's behind the kidnapping? Don't lie to me, Dan."

Dan looked around to see if anyone was watching. "Let me think."

"Quit stalling, old friend." When Dan didn't speak, Asa asked, "You still drive that 1967 Ford Cortina?"

Dan's eyes widened. "Now, Asa, don't touch my car. It's one of my prize possessions. You went with me to buy it from that old man living near Nonesuch. Remember?"

"Yeah, it was after you relocated here from New England. Why did you follow me from college to Lexington?"

Dan was aghast. "You suggested the Bluegrass. Even in college, you knew I loved horses. I like to gamble. I came because of the horse farms and the race track. I didn't follow you. You invited me to relocate to the Bluegrass. Besides you haven't lived here for years. Why do you care where I live? I don't bother anyone, least of all you."

"You're a horse bum. You gave up a lucrative job in computers to play the ponies."

"I'm good at the ponies, but I like to keep my hand in computers. It's amazing how far they've come since we were in school."

"Still a bookie?"

Dan gave Asa a sloppy grin. "I may make a bet for a friend now and then."

"You're wasting your life away sitting in that chair."

"So what! I can afford it." Dan twisted in his chair to face Asa. "I'm sorry that I kind of disappeared when things went bad for you with the government. You know I can't handle stress, but I was rooting for you."

"You didn't even call me, Dan. I thought you were my friend."

"Is this how you treat friends—interrogating and threatening them?"

"Let's say I am no longer your friend, Dan. You have now placed yourself on my enemy list." She leaned forward and whispered. "You know what I'm capable of."

Dan gulped. He remembered how Asa kicked those three frat boys' butts while he lay on the ground, covered in his own blood. After they ran away like scared jackrabbits, the frat boys found the tires slashed on their cars the next morning. In a few short hours, Asa had found out their names, their rides, and where they resided. The slashed tires were a warning not to retaliate against Dan or her.

After that, the three college boys crossed the street whenever they saw Dan or Asa. She could be terrifying even then.

"I am *your* friend, Asa. This is most unseemly of you."

"Regardless, I'm calling in my marker, kiddo."

Dan nodded. "If I do this for you, old college buddy, then my slate is clean."

"It depends on what you tell me and if it checks out."

"Where can I find you?"

"I'll find you. You practically live here, don't you, Danny boy?"

Dan took a deep breath. "Horses are my one addiction."

Asa grinned. "Just one addiction? How about being a clothes horse? Where's your usual Kiton cashmere suit?"

"I'm trying to break myself of the habit. My sartorial preferences were breaking the bank. That's why I'm wearing jeans."

Laughing, Asa said, "Those jeans cost more than an entire wardrobe for most people, and I won't even mention the loafers. You keep striving to be an average guy though."

Sensitive about his appearance, Dandy Dan sniffed the air in disdain. "What are you up to, Asa, since they drummed you out of the Secret Service?"

Asa drew back. She was as touchy about her firing as Daniel was about his clothes.

Dan was happy that he had pushed a red button. Asa was too smug for her own good. "I think we are done here for now. Goodbye Asa."

"Don't think about leaving town, Daniel. I have someone watching you. I'll expect some news from you in a couple of hours." She threw a burner phone at him. "Use it one time and then throw it in a storm drain."

Dan nervously looked around.

Asa was bluffing about having Dan watched, but her old friend didn't know that.

Yep, like her mother, Asa was a stinker.

9

A few hours later, Dandy Dan called.

Asa answered, "I'm listening."

"I was right. The kidnapping is a warning for Lady Elsmere. People don't like her push for reforms. A well-known player has been making veiled threats against her for months."

"Who told you this?"

"His ex-trainer who harbors a beef with the man. I had to slip him a grand. You better be good for it."

"I'm good. Now, who is it?"

"Ask the old woman yourself. Ask her who hates her guts the most. I can tell you the man has a son who's lonely. Go through him."

"Is the horse still alive?"

There was a click on the other line. Asa looked at her phone in disbelief. "Why the little turd!"

10

Lady Elsmere called about three in the afternoon. She wanted me to come over. I was in the midst of bottling Wildflower honey and said I would be over after I finished and had taken a shower. Bottling honey is a sticky affair, especially since I tend to drop bottles or fail to close the spigot quickly enough to stop the flow of thick tasty honey. In other words, I make a mess. The good thing is that when finished, I leave the door open to the honey house so the bees clean up everything—honey spilled on the floor, the honey dregs from the machine, and they even lick off microscopic bits of honey from the bottles. Presto—it's like magic.

    I finished my work, took a hot shower, put on clean clothes, and ambled over to Lady Elsmere's Big House. I found her on the patio smoking a cigarette.

    "You know you're not supposed to have those," I rebuked.

    "Leave me be, Josiah."

"What did you want, June? To tell me that Last Chance has been found?" I was hoping she had good news.

"If only." Lady Elsmere took a deep draw on her cigarette. "I have something I wanted to show you." She pointed toward the back kitchen door where Asa emerged carrying a tray of strawberry scones and a pot of tea with a bourbon bottle sticking out from her pocket.

"Hi, Mom." Asa placed the tray on the patio table and pulled the bottle out from her pocket.

"When did you get in?" I asked, astonished. As Asa sat in the chair next to me, I caught a whiff of horse sweat and manure.

"A day ago."

"Why didn't you come home?"

"I had to get some leads first. You distract me."

I rolled my eyes and said, "Oh, did you hear that, June? I am distracting."

Lady Elsmere barked, "Hush, Josiah. You two can argue later."

I shut my mouth, but pursed my lips directing my irritation at Asa. She ignored me.

"What did you find out, Asa?" Lady Elsmere asked.

"Well, Miss June, you've been stirring up the pot."

"What does that mean?" I asked, looking back and forth between them.

Lady Elsmere replied, "I think Asa is referring to

my legislative activism."

Asa said, "If you get your way, the racing world will change drastically. The powers that be in racing are afraid their pocketbooks will take a hit."

"There are too many accidents on the track, too many doped-up horses, too many injured jockeys, and too many abandoned race horses. Racing used to be the number one sport in America besides baseball. Everyone used to go to the races. Now the races have lost their glamour. No one wants to see horses spill on the track injuring jockeys. Something has got to change," Lady Elsmere countered.

"I don't disagree, Miss June, but many horse farms are just hanging on. People don't appreciate what it costs to run a horse farm and that includes Thoroughbreds, Saddlebreds, and Standardbreds. The money spent on the upkeep of fences alone threatens to squeeze the little guy out from the racing world. It's gotten so that only billionaires can own these farms. The average owner is being forced to sell their farms to developers who throw up subdivisions and tacky strip malls. What you're proposing would bring about the loss of more farms and horse people finding themselves in the unemployment line," Asa retorted heatedly.

I held up my hands. "Whoa there, ladies. We are all working for the same cause. Let's simmer down."

Asa looked embarrassed which was rare for her.

"I'm sorry, Miss June. I forgot that I'm here to find Last Chance."

"June, if you can't get the law changed, would you still allow Last Chance to run in the Kentucky Derby at three years of age?" I asked.

Lady Elsmere nodded. "Call me a hypocrite if you like, but I am winding down, girls. I would take that chance. I want to have a Kentucky Derby winner before I die—God forgive me."

Pouring three cups of tea each with a splash of bourbon, I said, "Let's not get so maudlin. You're not dead yet, June, and most horses start racing at two years old and retire to stud without an incident." I turned to Asa. "What did you find out?"

"I had two people tell me that the kidnapping was a warning for you to stop meddling, Miss June. People don't like it when you mess with their pocketbooks."

Lady Elsmere looked surprised. "It had nothing to do with jealousy? My rivals?"

Asa answered, "Maybe a little of both. There was a tip the syndicate might be involved, but I think the danger is closer to home."

"Is the colt still alive?" June asked.

Asa shrugged. "I don't know."

Lady Elsmere recounted, "You're too young to remember this, Asa, but the most famous horse kidnapping was Shergar. He was on par with Secretariat with a stud fee was $105,000 dollars. He was standing at stud in Ireland when he disappeared in 1983."

Asa whistled. "That was a lot of moola in the early 80s."

Lady Elsmere continued, "Shergar and his groom, Jim Fitzgerald, were kidnapped at gunpoint. The kidnappers let Jim Fitzgerald go eventually, saying they were holding the horse for ransom."

"What happened?" Asa asked.

"It was believed the Irish Republican Army stole the horse. They needed money for arms and weapons, but they made one mistake—they let Shergar's handler go. Without Jim Fitzgerald, they couldn't control the agitated stallion. In the last contact with the negotiators, the kidnappers said there had been an accident and the horse was dead. They never called back again. No one ever found the body of Shergar, and the kidnappers were never caught."

Asa suggested, "Perhaps they lied and sold the horse."

Lady Elsmere took a long drag on her cigarette before putting it out. "No, that wouldn't have worked. Shergar was too well-known internationally. The horse died in an accident or was shot on purpose because the heat on the case was too hot. We'll never know."

"Do you think Last Chance is dead?"

"Asa, if Last Chance is not dead, he will be soon. Foals his age need their mothers. I doubt the kidnappers know the correct way to care for a colt without a dam. He must be found within the next several days," Lady Elsmere explained.

Asa took a sip of her tea. "And you've received no phone calls or letters demanding ransom?"

Lady Elsmere shook her head.

I said, "I think that proves Last Chance was taken to punish June and not for monetary reward."

Asa replied, "Maybe. Maybe not."

I said, "Where do we go from here, Asa?"

Asa took a deep breath. "I was given a tip on where to look, but you must put up the money for my operatives and their legal fees and bail if they get caught. Do you agree, June?"

"Of course, Asa. Money is no object."

"Now give me the name of your biggest enemy in the horse business. The one person who really hates your guts."

Lady Elsmere answered without hesitation. "I don't even have to think about it. Logan J. Kilkorn."

"Has he been in contact?"

"No."

"When was the last time you spoke with him or his associates?"

"It would have been when I testified before the Racing Commission on the issue of abandoning retired Thorougbreds or selling them to slaughter houses."

I said, "Kentucky has a law banning the slaughtering of Thoroughbreds for meat."

Lady Elsmere replied, "Owners ship their horses to states that don't have the ban."

Asa asked, "What happened when you testified, Miss June?"

"Logan was appointed to speak on behalf of the opposing side. He lost control though. Logan got tongue-tied when I rebutted some of his arguments and blurted out some very not-so-nice epitaphs at me, causing him to lose credibility before the Racing Commission. His reputation took a hit. I haven't talked to him since."

"That was over two years ago," I said. "Since then Logan has been banned from racing when one of his stable hands got caught doping a competitor's horse."

Asa looked at her mother. "So, he likes to play rough with other people's horses. Tell me one thing. Does he have a son?"

Lady Elsmere replied, "Yes, and I hear he is in the midst of a divorce, and it is a nasty one by all accounts."

Asa looked at the two of us and announced, "I think I'll pay a call on Logan J. Kilkorn."

"I like the sound of that," Lady Elsmere said, her eyes twinkling.

The three of us raised our tea cups and clinked them.

Logan J. Kilkorn didn't know it yet, but a tornado was coming his way!

11

Logan J. Kilkorn had a son about Asa's age—maybe a little younger and who was going through a divorce. One thing Asa knew was that men loved to talk about themselves and complain about their exes. It was easy enough to find out his favorite watering hole—the Chevy Chase Inn, one of the oldest dive bars in Lexington.

Asa strolled in wearing tight black jeans and a silver top displaying ample cleavage with her brunette hair cascading softly over her shoulders. She seated herself at the bar and ordered a white wine spritzer, surveying the patrons while draping her bag over the back of the bar stool. Needless to say, heads turned.

A middle-aged, balding man ambled over to her. "May I buy you a drink?"

"No, thank you. I'm waiting for my husband."

"Oh."

"No really, thank you. It was nice of you to ask."

The man leaned against the bar. His hands looked

sweaty. "Well, maybe I should keep you company until he gets here."

Asa smiled. "I don't think you want to do that. My husband's a cop."

"Oh."

"See you around." Asa got up and sat in a booth, nursing her drink. After forty-five minutes, Micah Kilkorn walked in and sat at the bar, ordering a vodka and cranberry juice. Asa was relieved Micah was somewhat nice-looking and didn't have a potbelly flopping over his belt. He was wearing high-quality clothes and had recently shaved. She caught a whiff of his aftershave lotion. Sizing Kilkorn up, Asa noticed he still had his boyish looks although she detected a little weakening under the chin. She thought Micah was awfully young for that, but maybe he drank too much.

She got up and put some coins in the jukebox, making sure she was noticed. Micah didn't follow her with his eyes like most of the men in the bar did, but she was sure he saw her. She went over to the bar and stood next to him, looking at his drink. "What are you drinking?"

"Vodka and cranberry juice," he replied.

"No bourbon?"

"Don't like bourbon," Micah answered.

Asa thumbed at his drink to the bartender and said, "I'll have what he's having."

The bartender answered, "Sure thing."

"Nice night, isn't it?" Asa inquired of Micah.

Micah looked at Asa squarely and said, "Are you trying to pick me up?"

"Is it working?"

"It might. Want to tell me your name?"

"Billy with a y," Asa lied.

"Billy with a y? That's how boys spell it."

"It's my name."

"Are you a boy?"

Asa leaned over a bit showing off more of her cleavage. "Do I look like a boy?"

"Just checking."

"What's your name?"

"Micah."

Asa extended her right hand. "Nice to meet you, Mr. Micah."

Micah shook her hand. "Is there a last name after Billy?"

Asa teased, "Aren't you forward? You haven't even bought me dinner yet and here you are asking personal questions like that."

Micah motioned to the bartender and asked, "Is the kitchen still open?"

"They're cleaning up now, but I'm sure the chili is still hot."

Micah turned to Asa. "You like chili?"

Asa requested, "Can I get some hot sauce and crackers with it?"

The bartender replied, "You bet. Micah?"

"I'll have what the lady's having and put it on my tab, Sid."

Asa picked up the vodka and cranberry drink placed before her, hopping off her stool. "Want to sit at a booth? We'll be more comfortable."

"Sure."

They turned around but saw all the booths were taken. Asa grinned and slid back onto the bar stool. "I guess we're laying claim to this piece of real estate."

Micah scooted his bar stool closer to Asa. "Are you new in town? I haven't seen you before."

"I came back to visit my mother. She's been having health problems."

"Sorry to hear that. Do you always go to bars without your husband?"

Asa pointed to her empty ring finger. "What is this? Twenty questions?"

"Sorry."

"You apologize a lot."

"Sorry." Micah grinned sheepishly.

Asa flipped her hair back. "I'll tell you. I used to come to this bar a lot when I was in college."

"You went to school at UK?"

Asa nodded and lied, "Yep."

"I went to school here, too. What was your major?"

"There you go again. Being personal. Just be friendly, Micah, if that is your real name."

The bartender brought two large bowls of chili with all the fixings—extra onions, cheese, and sour cream.

Micah thumbed at the bartender. "Sid, tell this lovely lady my name."

Sid answered, "He's Micah Kilkorn. Do you need anything else, folks?"

"No, we're fine. Thank you," Asa said, pouring hot sauce on her chili.

Micah said, "Hey, watch that hot sauce. How am I gonna kiss you with your mouth on fire?"

"First of all, who says I'll allow you to kiss me, and what's wrong with being on fire?"

"You are one beautiful dangerous lady," Micah said, his eyes glittering.

"You have no idea," Asa replied, blowing him a kiss. "Come on, now. Let's eat this chili. It smells divine."

"Sure. We'll both have bad breath then." Micah crumbled crackers in his chili. "What do you do, Billy with a y?"

"I appraise art for insurance companies."

"Oh, really. That must be interesting."

"I like it. What do you do?"

"I'm in the equine business."

"Who isn't in the Bluegrass," Asa replied.

"My family owns a horse farm."

"Sure, they do."

"No, really. We do."

"Then you must be a trust fund baby."

Micah bristled a bit. "My family is well-off, but I work just like every other Joe."

"Sorry, I didn't mean to be rude."

Micah relented. "How can I be angry with such a beautiful woman?"

"Do you live on the farm in a big antebellum home like Tara in *Gone with the Wind*?"

"There you go again. Being snotty. What have you got against rich people?"

Asa giggled. "Only that I'm not one of them."

Micah smirked. "If you must know I live in the pool house behind my parents' home, and yes, it's a big antebellum house with the Corinthian columns and wide porticos."

"Okay. I'll back off. Let's eat and talk about more pleasant things."

"I'm fine with that."

Nodding, Asa plowed into her food. She was really hungry and ate the chili with gusto.

Micah dropped a paper napkin and bent over in his chair to retrieve it.

Asa took advantage of this distraction to put a few drops into Micah's chili from a little vial she had hidden in her cleavage. "Here, Micah, use a clean napkin. Don't use that one. It's touched the floor." She pulled several from the napkin dispenser on the bar.

"Thanks," he said, wiping his mouth with a fresh

napkin. He took several more bites of the chili.

They chitchatted for several minutes until Micah winced.

Asa asked, "What's wrong?"

"I don't know. I suddenly feel nauseous and light-headed."

"You don't look so well. You're sweating and your color is off." Asa motioned to the bartender.

"Maybe I have food poisoning?" Micah clutched his stomach in pain.

"I think I should take you to the hospital," Asa said.

"No. NO! I just need to get home."

The bartended strode over. "Micah. You don't look so good. What's going on?"

"I think I have food poisoning," Micah complained.

Asa reiterated, "I had the same chili and I feel fine. I think you really need to see a doctor."

"I just want to go home. No doctors." Micah grimaced again in obvious pain.

Asa asked the bartender, "Where does he live?"

"On a horse farm out Parkers Mill Road. You can't miss it. Big metal gate with the initials LK."

"Okay, I'll take him home."

"That might be best. I'll call his home and let them know he's coming."

Micah reached up and tugged on Sid's arm. "Don't. Please. I don't want my old man to know I'm under the weather. Okay?"

"I think I should call your old man, Micah," Sid said.

"No, please. This would give him one more reason to call me an idiot. He's always on my case."

"Sure, Micah. Anything you say."

Asa took note about Micah and his father. "Can you help me get him into his car?" Asa asked, grabbing her bag.

Sid reached into the booth, pulling Micah up and helping him to his car. Before Sid slid Micah in the passenger seat, Asa rooted through his pockets and retrieved the 1962 Alpha Romeo Spider blue convertible's keys. He didn't notice Asa putting on a pair of black leather gloves.

"Thanks, Sid," Asa said getting in the driver's seat of the sports car after putting her bag in the trunk. "I'll make sure I get him home."

At that moment, Micah leaned over and vomited on the pavement. Disgusted, Sid gladly shut Micah's door. "Good luck, lady," he said, before walking away.

Asa turned on the convertible and pulled out of the parking lot as Micah slid down in his seat, groaning. She patted him on the shoulder. "Don't worry, Micah. It will be all over in a few hours. You'll be good as new."

It wasn't long before Asa was racing down a winding country lane toward Parkers Mill Road.

12

Asa exited the car and managed to get Micah into the pool house where she deposited him in the bathroom. She pulled off Micah's soiled pants and threw them in the laundry basket before he began hugging the toilet. This gave her plenty of time to go through his phone, make copies of his keys with a new app, and downloaded his computer files, sending the information to an operative waiting for the information. Then she went through his desk and searched the pool house.

Hearing Micah call for her, Asa went back to the bathroom and helped him into the shower. "Don't worry, Micah. You're not going to remember a thing about this. Besides, you don't have anything I haven't seen before." She stripped him naked and made sure he was clean before turning off the water. After drying Micah off, Asa found a pair of soft athletic shorts for him before putting the groggy and exhausted man to bed. "Nighty-night, Micah. Go to sleep. I've got more work to do."

Asa pulled a pair of night goggles with a Go-Pro camera attached to the side, and a walkie talkie from her bag, tied the bag around her waist, and turned off the lights. She silently left the pool house, taking care no one was around and searched the property. It was very difficult as there were security cameras everywhere—the kind that tripped peoples' phones, so she had to work fast. Sooner or later, security would be summoned.

Hurrying to the horse barns, she checked all the stalls. Finding no sign of Last Chance, she made her way along a spring running through a pasture. Close by was an abandoned early nineteenth-century farm house with a separate brick root cellar, which Asa had discovered from studying satellite photos of the property earlier that day. The house and cellar were surrounded by a fence with the metal gate left open.

The house was full of hay bales. It was not unusual for farms to store additional hay or feed in old buildings if the roofs were good. However, it was unusual to find horse droppings in a house. Asa took a deep breath. She was close.

Surely, they would not have put that foal in that damp root cellar. Asa couldn't fathom that. Still, she had to check. It only took her a few seconds to reach the root cellar. It was a large brick dome sticking out of the ground with spring water running underneath the cellar floor. The cellar was built over the stream to keep items cool in the summer. Asa studied the steps leading down to the door.

Good Lord! There was a padlock on the door! The colt had to be in the cellar. Asa was careful going down the slimy, mossy steps. She couldn't afford an accident now. Reaching the door, she tried pushing it. It was too sturdy to knock down. Asa pressed her ear against the door and heard a small whinny. The colt was inside!

Pulling out her walkie talkie, she said, "I found him. Be ready."

A voice replied, "They're on to you. The house just lit up like a Christmas tree."

"Copy."

As there was no reason to be quiet now, Asa picked up a loose brick and banged away at the lock until it broke. Throwing open the door, she stared at an agitated colt neighing and pacing back and forth in fear. "Hey there, little fellow. I'm gonna take you back to your mom." Asa turned her head as she heard shouts in the distance.

"Look, I know you're scared, and I don't have time to make friends with you. You just have to trust me. I am going to carry you up those stairs, so don't kick me or we will both fall. Neither one of us can afford a broken leg." Asa pulled a small blanket from her bag.

Asa cornered the colt. He struggled for a second until Asa put the blanket over his eyes. "Oh jeez, you weigh a ton," Asa muttered, picking the colt up. She was glad she lifted weights as part of her training.

Still the bandaged wound on her side felt like it had opened. Asa felt a little faint, but gritted her teeth. No time to think about that now. She gingerly climbed up the root cellar's steps making sure she was not in danger of slipping. The steps were slowing her down.

Breathing heavily, Asa made it to the top and put the colt down while clutching his mane. He tried to buck Asa, but she held fast. Going into her bag again, she pulled out a halter and a lead. "I came prepared, little guy. We're going home."

Asa looked up after hearing car motors. Lights were coming toward her across the pasture. She hurried to put on the halter while the colt tossed his head, fighting every step of the way. "Don't argue with me. We've just got seconds."

Just then, a black truck with a horse trailer crashed through the wooden fences surrounding the pasture where the root cellar was. The truck stopped about ten feet from the cellar. A man jumped out of the passenger's side and ran to open the trailer.

Asa pulled the colt over to the trailer where the man picked up the horse and carried him inside. Asa closed the back of the trailer and jumped in the passenger's seat throwing her bag on the floor. "HIT IT!"

The truck and trailer busted through another series of fences onto Parkers Mill Road. A minute later two SUV's went through the opening in the fence, following them.

Asa poked her head out of the window watching the SUV's swerving behind them. "They're gaining."

"There's only so fast I can go with this trailer," the operative said. "We'll be there in a minute."

"I should have let the air out of everyone's tires."

Asa's operative shook his head. "You would have been caught for sure."

"We're almost there. No matter what. Keep going."

Fifty seconds later, Asa's employee swerved through an open gate into a pasture where five cars were parked with their lights on in a line guarding another horse trailer.

Asa grabbed her wounded side as her man sped into the field and slammed on the truck's brakes. When she pulled her hand away, it was covered in blood, which had seeped through her clothes. "Park beside the other trailer," she ordered. The foal had to be reunited with his dam before anything else.

The operative drove slowly and stopped next to the other trailer.

Asa pressed against her wound trying to stop the bleeding and bit her lip. When she moved to open the door, Asa couldn't push through the agonizing pain, only then realizing she must have done more than just open her bullet wound.

Asa decided to sit in the truck for now. There was time to tend to her when Jean Harlow and her foal were brought back together.

The horses had to come first.

13

Lady Elsmere, Shaneika Mary Todd, Charles Dupuy, Mike Conner, and a vet waited with two security guards with guns. The vet, Mike, and Shaneika ran to the back of the foal's trailer as Asa's man jumped out with the foal.

The pursing SUV's slowed down, but passed by when they saw the knot of people holding their phones up filming. Too many witnesses. Too many things could go wrong. Mike jogged over to the gate post where he had placed a camera Asa had given him. He was sure he had captured the vehicles' license plates numbers. He closed the gate and ran back to assist with backing Jean Harlow out from her trailer. She excitedly sniffed the air and whinnied. She knew her baby was close by.

Last Chance whinnied back upon hearing his mother. It was all Mike could do to lead an excited Jean Harlow out of the trailer while Asa's man held open the trailer door. Asa's other crew member held Last

Chance from bolting. Finally, he picked up the colt, which was kicking and neighing, and carried the colt over to Jean Harlow, letting her smell him. The colt became too agitated, so the operative put him on the ground and stood back. This was the decisive moment.

Shaneika squeezed Lady Elsmere's hand in anticipation. Would Jean Harlow accept Last Chance?

The colt sniffed as Jean Harlow nervously sidestepped away.

Mike held tightly on Jean Harlow's lead rope, slipping her some sweet feed with his other hand. "Whoa, girl. Be nice, now." Jean Harlow munched on the sweet feed, keeping a wild eye on the colt. This little creature smelled like her baby, but she was not so sure.

The colt eagerly butted his mother's side with his muzzle, searching for her teat. Jean Harlow snorted and tossed her head. Mike gave her more sweet feed while the vet came over to grab her halter. Last Chance latched on to a teat causing Jean Harlow to kick and stomp her back left hoof.

Mike asked the vet. "Can you give the mother something to calm her?"

"You gotta let nature takes its course, Mike," the vet answered. "Just talk to her. You raised her. She'll listen to you."

Mike stroked Jean Harlow's muzzle and behind the ears. "This is your foal. It's Last Chance. He needs to nurse. Be a good mommy."

Last Chance tried to latch on a teat again. This time Jean Harlow bucked. The vet pulled the colt away. Mike walked around with Jean Harlow to see if the colt would follow.

Shaneika murmured a prayer.

The colt followed the mare.

Shaneika clasped her hands in thanks.

Lady Elsmere sighed and murmured to Charles, "I need a drink and a bed. I'm too old for this."

Mike let go of the halter and walked away.

To everyone's disbelief, Jean Harlow trotted away from the colt.

The vet carefully watched Last Chance. "I'm going to give them about fifteen minutes. If Jean Harlow doesn't let him nurse, then I'm gonna give him a bottle and call it a night."

Disappointed, Lady Elsmere asked, "How does he look?"

"A little thin, but other than that, okay. I need to take some blood samples before I give him a clean bill of health. After I'm through with him, what happens?"

"We'll take them back to the farm and try again to unite them. If Jean Harlow doesn't take to Last Chance, we have a surrogate mare for him. Whichever mare Last Chance ends up with will be moved to a secret location until this mess is cleared up," Lady Elsmere answered. "We'll have no more of this chicanery."

"Why weren't the cops called when you learned of

Last Chance's location?" the vet asked. "Seems to me all this cloak and dagger business should have been handled by the police and not your people. You found your horse, but there's still a matter of Juan Gomez's murder."

"I'm well aware of that," Lady Elsmere shot back.

Overhearing mention of the police, Asa motioned to her operatives.

"Yeah, Boss?"

"We need to disappear before the police are called. I don't trust that vet to keep his mouth shut. Leave the truck and trailer here. We can take one of Lady Elsmere's vehicles back. Help me to a car."

One of the operatives studied Asa as she struggled to get out of the truck. "You're bleeding!"

"HUSH! Get me into a car and let's go."

"Stay in the truck. I'm taking you to the emergency room."

"NO! NO HOPITALS! I can't afford to have this wound reported."

The operative opened his mouth to reply, but Asa tumbled out before the man could speak or catch her.

The last thing Asa remembered was the sweet smell of bluegrass as she hit the ground and her man calling for help. Then everything blacked out.

14

You know it's never good when the phone rings late at night. A chill went up my spine as I answered the phone. "Hello?"

"Josiah. This is Shaneika."

"What's happened?" I raised myself up on my elbows while Baby bounced his head on my mattress, trying to get my attention. I pushed his big head away as I sat up.

"Asa is in the hospital. You'd better come."

"How bad is it?"

"We don't know yet. She's in surgery."

"Who *is* we?"

"Charles and I are at the hospital. Lady Elsmere went home with Mike."

"Went home from where? What were you all doing?"

"The less you know, the better."

"Does it have to do with your colt?"

"The less you know—the better."

"It did, didn't it?"

There was silence from Shaneika.

"You know something, Shaneika. I don't really give a damn if you got your horse back or not. You'd better have some answers for me when I get there." I slammed the phone receiver down.

I was so angry that my daughter might have risked her life for that foal I could have spit cotton. All of this nonsense over a potential Kentucky Derby winner. Someone was going to get a piece of my mind when I got to the hospital.

Now, where were my pants!

15

Matt, my best friend who lived on my property, drove me to the hospital. We made a pit stop at the Lady Elsmere's to drop off his daughter, Emmeline, with Bess and Amelia after we saw the lights on at the Big House. The two sisters were very tight lipped about what had happened, but didn't fight me about taking care of the baby. I think they were expecting us to drop her off.

I had met Matt years ago at a party where he was challenged to a movie bet. What was the command Kentuckian Patricia Neal gave the robot, Gort, in the sci-fi movie *The Day the Earth Stood Still?*

I leaned over and whispered in Matt's ear, "It was "Klaatu barada nikto."

Matt won some money and bragging rights, and I had won a devoted friend. We've been stuck together like glue ever since then. Oh, we've had our ups-and-downs, but we made an agreement to butt out of each other's personal lives. It's been smooth sailing since then—okay, you caught me. Most of the time it is smooth sailing. Matt's been shot because of me, but that's in the past.

I love Matt and it wouldn't take much to make me fall in love with him. He's gorgeous for one thing—over six feet tall, wavy raven hair, patrician features, and blue eyes. He's a tax attorney and honest to the point of being boring. However, where his personal life is concerned—don't turn your back on him. He'll cheat on any "beloved" if he just sniffs something more interesting. It doesn't bode well for any adult falling in love with Matt. I warn him all the time that he's going to end up old and alone if he doesn't change his ways.

Matt has been better with his wicked ways since Emmeline was born. He is besotted with his only child and is a good father by all accounts. I have hopes that Matt will mellow into a mature male who has cultivated high standards regarding his love life. I'll keep you posted on Matt's development.

It took twenty-five minutes to reach the hospital. All the while, I was biting my bottom lip and clutching one of Emmeline's stuffed animals. I wished Baby was with me. I never realized how much I depended on that dog until he wasn't with me.

We came to the main entrance of the hospital in an abrupt stop. I quickly jumped out and ran inside while Matt parked the car. I called Shaneika from the hospital foyer. She answered her phone.

"Where?"

"Third floor. Waiting room on the left."

I called Matt and told him where I would be and then ran to catch the elevator. I was worried sick and felt as though I might vomit. Asa was all the family I had left. The thought of being alone frightened me. Let's face reality. Lady Elsmere would die sooner or later—more sooner than later. Matt would eventually buy his own house and move away. Oh, yeah, I had lots of friends, but no one else who makes that deep bone connection—know what I mean? Yeah, I was afraid for my beautiful daughter and for myself. I think *terrified* was a better word.

Shaneika was waiting for me at the elevator.

"Where is she?"

"She's still in recovery, but the nurse said she's doing fine. The doctor said he would come out and talk to you."

"Is she going to be okay?"

"The nurse seemed to think so."

"What happened?"

"That's a little fuzzy. We don't know. We don't even know what caused the injury. All we know is Asa was bleeding from her side and passed out."

"Did she have any operatives with her?"

Shaneika took a deep breath, hesitating before speaking. "Yes, but they seemed as confused as we did."

"I want to talk with them."

"That's gonna be hard, Josiah. As soon as we loaded Asa in a car to take her to the hospital, they stole one of our vehicles and lit out. We have no idea where they are."

"I hate you right now, Shaneika."

Shaneika looked pained. "That's fear talking, Josiah."

"Maybe so, but I hate your guts right now."

"Let's concentrate on getting Asa well, and then you can chew me out again. Deal?"

"Deal." I stomped into the reception room where Charles stood waiting. I sat down not speaking a word to him. He sat beside me and took my hand in his large, calloused one. We sat holding hands like old comrades who had been beaten down by too much sorrow and defeat.

Shaneika sat on the opposite side and thumbed through outdated magazines.

The three of us waited in an uncomfortable silence.

16

A doctor, about my daughter's age, strode into the waiting room. She looked tired and out of patience with life. I guess she had witnessed too much. "Mrs. Reynolds?"

I stood, as did Charles and Shaneika. "That's me. I'm Mrs. Reynolds."

She glanced at my African-American comrades. I could tell she tried to make our connection with one another, but was really too tired to be curious. "Is Asa Reynolds your daughter?"

"Yes, she is. How is she? May I see her?"

"She's doing fine considering."

"What does that mean, Doctor?" Shaneika asked.

"And you are?"

"I'm her attorney."

"I can only speak with family. I'm sure you understand, counselor." The doctor pulled me aside. "Your daughter is seriously injured."

"From tonight?"

"Yes, but her initial injuries are much older. It's seems she had more serious trauma previously. Do you know the name of the doctor who treated her?"

"I'm sorry. I didn't even know she had been injured before this."

"Do you know what she was doing tonight?"

I shook my head. "No. I just got a call that she was taken to the hospital and told to come."

"I can't go into her medical issues, but she is going to need lots of rest and care. Does Miss Reynolds live here? It is Miss, isn't it?"

"Asa has an apartment in New York and one in London. She is divorced."

The doctor raised an eyebrow. "What does she do for a living?"

I blanched and gave the standard answer. "She's an insurance art investigator."

"That means what?"

"She investigates international art thefts and also does appraisals."

"That sounds dangerous."

"It can be."

"Was she working on a case tonight?"

"Doctor, I'm sorry, but I don't know. If Asa was, she couldn't tell me. Professional ethics."

The doctor peered closer at me. "Art. That seems to ring a bell with me. Did you ever teach at UK?"

"I was a history professor for the art department."

"I think I was in one of your classes. Yes, I really think I was. I remember. You were Professor Reynolds."

"Can we get back to my daughter, Doctor—?" I looked for a badge.

"McGhee. Doctor Ariel McGhee."

"I would like to see my daughter."

"Miss Reynolds is still in recovery. It will be an hour or so before we move her to a room. That will be 314. You can wait in there if you like, but we'll need for you to fill out some paperwork before you do. Just go down to the Admitting Office and help them out with the paperwork."

"I shall. Thank you."

The doctor gave a fleeting smile and left.

I turned to Shaneika and Charles. "I'm staying but you two go home and get some rest."

"I'm staying," Shaneika said.

The elevator door opened and Matt got off. He walked over to us. "What's the news?"

Shaneika said, "Josiah was in the middle of telling Charles and me to go home."

"I don't think that's wise, Jo," Matt said, giving me the stink eye.

I gave him the stink eye right back. "You three have to work tomorrow. You still have time to get home and get some shuteye before work. It only makes sense."

Matt replied, "I don't feel right about leaving you here alone."

"I'll be fine. You three have places to be in a few hours." I could see the three were not convinced. "Charles, you have to check on the old woman. Shaneika, you have to be in court tomorrow. Matt, you have to pick up Emmeline and be at work tomorrow by nine. I'll be fine. The only thing I ask is that you take Baby to stay at the Big House until I get home."

"No problem. I'll do that, Josiah," Charles agreed. "I'll get him as soon as I get back to the farm. He'll be fine staying with us."

I gave a sigh of relief. "Thank you. I appreciate that. I'll call as soon as I know something."

Matt pointed a finger at me. "You better. Come on, Shaneika. I'll walk you to your car."

Shaneika gave me a sympathetic look before following Matt to the elevator as Charles pressed my hand one last time. "Everything will be fine, Josiah. Trust in the Lord."

I nodded but I wasn't so sure. It seemed God has favorites, granting his mercy helter-skelter.

My problem was I didn't know if I made his favorite list. I was pretty sure Asa wasn't on it.

17

An hour later, Asa was wheeled in on a gurney. I jumped to my feet when they brought her in. She looked terrible, but managed to grunt, "Mom."

"I'm here, Asa. I'm here." I stood in a corner until the nurse and orderlies scooted Asa onto her bed and finished hooking her up to a monitoring machine and IV's. I thanked them before they left the room.

The nurse said, "I'll be checking on her every hour if you want to go home and get some rest."

"I'll stay if I'm not in the way."

"Suit yourself. I'm right down the hall if you need anything."

"Thank you. You're very kind."

"It's what we do," the nurse said, giving me a friendly nod. She shut the door quietly.

I pulled my chair over to Asa's bed. "Asa, can you hear me?"

Asa flicked a finger.

"Do you need anything?"

"Cold."

I found a blanket in the bureau and threw it on her. "Go to sleep, Asa. I'm not leaving."

She muttered, "So sorry, Mom."

"We'll talk about it later."

The nurse knocked on the door and stepped inside. "There is a Detective Drake and Detective Kelly outside. They say they need to speak with Miss Reynolds."

"I'll see them." I followed the nurse into the hallway. "What's up, guys? Why are you here?"

Kelly stood behind Drake and looked beseechingly at me. I knew he was here to see how Asa was doing. I wish that flame between Kelly and Asa would flutter out. Kelly would be much happier. I know his wife would be more content with her marriage.

Drake answered, "We're here to question Asa about the murder of Juan Gomez. We think she might have some information concerning it."

I replied, "Asa wasn't even in town when Mr. Gomez was killed. What could she possibly know?"

"There was a little incident on Parkers Mill Road tonight. She have anything to do with that?"

"I don't know what you're talking about, Drake. What incident?"

"Logan Kilkorn says someone trespassed on his farm tonight and stole one of his foals. He thinks Lady Elsmere might have something to do with it."

I snapped, "Then you'll have to ask Lady Elsmere. Now, if you would excuse me, I want to tend to my daughter."

"How is she?" Kelly asked, stepping forward.

"I don't really know. They just brought her in. She's still reeling from the sedation."

Drake shifted his weight to one foot and asked, "Her doc called us and said she had a gunshot injury that reopened. Know anything about that?"

I must have looked surprised as Drake gave me a break. He knew that I knew doctors have to report bullet holes, stab wounds, and abuse to the police, so my shocked look informed Drake that I didn't know about her injuries.

Drake said, "Looks like we can't talk to her tonight, but we'll be back tomorrow. Tell Miss Reynolds when she wakes up."

"I'll give her the news."

"Until tomorrow then." Drake tipped the brim of his hat and walked away.

Kelly stayed for just a few seconds longer. "Is Asa out of danger?"

"I don't know. I hope so. I am as much in the dark as you are. I swear it."

"KELLY!" Drake barked holding the elevator for his junior detective.

"I'll see you later," Kelly said quickly before joining his partner.

Going back into Asa's room, I was very confused, but curious about Logan Kilkorn's accusation. I looked at Asa fitfully sleeping. "What have you been up to, daughter of mine?" I murmured. "Doesn't sound good."

I gingerly pulled away the blankets and lifted her hospital gown. Asa was covered with fading bruises and new deep blue ones. There were several old scars around her left shoulder and a large bandage covering what must have been the bullet wound. "Oh, child, what have you done to your beautiful body?" I could have wept as I replaced her gown and blankets.

I went back to my chair and tried to sleep, determined to get some answers tomorrow. The night stretched out before me like a long, tangled, black ribbon.

It was lonely listening to the beep of the monitor and Asa's ragged breathing.

I thought to myself—*would the morning ever come?*

18

I must have finally fallen asleep as I jerked in my chair when a new nurse came into the room. She switched the IV bags and checked the monitor.

"What time is it?" I asked, seeing light coming through the window blinds.

"Six-forty," the nurse replied. "Been here all night?"

I nodded my head while stretching my arms. "How is she doing?" I asked referring to Asa.

"Steady. They'll probably let her go tomorrow morning. She slept through the night."

"Good. Good."

"Why don't you go home, get some rest, and freshen up? She'll be okay."

I replied, "A hot shower sounds nice. I think that's in store for me this morning."

The nurse checked Asa's vitals and typed the info into a tablet. Not like the old days where relatives could snoop and read the patient's clipboard info left hanging at the end of their bed. I still didn't know exactly what was wrong with Asa.

After the nurse left, I rinsed my mouth, washed my face, and combed my hair. I still looked a mess. The nurse was right. I needed to go home and clean up. Pulling out my phone, I searched for the Uber app to request a ride.

"Mom?"

I looked over at Asa whose eyes were fluttering. Patting her arm, I said, "I'm here, Asa. What can I get for you?"

"Where am I?"

"You're in the hospital. The doctor says you have some sort of gunshot wound. Is that true, Asa?"

"I'm in a hospital?"

"Yes. Shaneika said you passed out last night. Want to tell me about what you and Shaneika were doing?"

Asa reached for the IV needle, pulling it from her arm. "I've got to get out of here."

Alarmed, I pushed Asa down. "What are you doing? You've got to stay in the hospital!"

Asa slapped my hands away. "You don't understand. I can't stay. I can't be implicated in any police matter. I'm on the lam myself."

I froze. "What did you say?"

"I was hiding out in Key Largo. I thought I could sneak in and out of Kentucky without being detected. Do the police know I'm here?"

"Yes. They want to talk with you today."

Asa swung her legs over the edge of the bed and sat up unsteadily. "Then my location has been compromised. If I get sucked into this affair, I'll lose my job and my license."

"I don't understand, Asa. You said something about being on the lam."

"I don't have time to explain. I've got the leave this hospital. You've got to help me. NOW!"

"Okay. Okay. Let me think."

"Where are my clothes?"

"Probably cut off in the ER last night."

"Get your car and meet me at the employee's entrance."

"I don't have my car. Matt drove me. I was going to take an Uber home."

"Get me some sort of transportation. I need wheels."

I ran out into the hallway, looking for a wheelchair. Racing back to Asa's room with one, I called Shaneika, leaving a message to meet us at the side entrance. When I entered the room again, I found the bed empty only to discover Asa behind the door holding a bedpan over her head, ready to strike.

"For God's Sake, Asa. You're acting like a crazy person."

Asa didn't reply but sat down in the wheelchair.

I propped open the door and wheeled her out.

"Where are you going?" a practical nurse asked,

running into us in the hallway.

"My daughter woke up and says she's famished. Since dinner is not for a bit, I thought I could take her to the cafeteria." I gave the nurse my best TV mom smile.

Asa chimed in, saying she could do with a little soup. "We won't be long. I think I need a change of pace for a few minutes."

The day nurse seemed suspicious but acquiesced. "Please no more than thirty minutes. Don't let her reach for anything. It might open the stitches again."

I said, "We'll be careful, I promise."

"Oh, another thing. They still need to see someone in the Admitting Office to fill out the paperwork."

"Sure thing. I'll get right on it," I lied.

She looked at Asa. "Where are your IV's?"

Asa replied, "The doctor said I didn't need them anymore and took me off them."

"That's curious. He didn't mention it to us."

Asa shrugged.

"I'm surprised you feel well enough to get about. Remember, just soup or Jell-O now. They have a wonderful minestrone and tomato bisque today. It will be easy on your system."

"I'll make sure she stays on her diet," I said to the nurse, pushing the elevator button.

The nurse heard her name called from the nurses' desk and walked down the hallway. The elevator opened. Instead of getting on, I pushed a button for the door to close and then wheeled Asa down the hall away far away from the nurses' desk. I went down several hallways and found an elevator not in use. I took it to the women's section on the second floor where they did mammograms. The hospital proper and the women's area were connected by a bridge, which contained bathrooms not usually engaged. I hid Asa in the handicapped stall and then went to guard outside on a waiting bench. I could look down into the foyer and see who was milling about on the first floor.

I saw Detective Drake and Detective Kelly come in the front door. They both looked very serious.

Uh oh!

19

It would take Drake and Kelly time to track us down. They had to go to the third floor, question the right nurse who knew where we were, go to the cafeteria, and then start searching for us in earnest. I looked at the time on my phone. Where was Shaneika?

My phone rang. Finally! "Yes."

"I'm at the side entrance."

I hung up and gathered Asa still hiding in the handicapped bathroom stall. I know I'll look back at this and find it humorous, but I sure didn't at the moment. Asa put on my sunglasses as I wheeled her to the first floor, down some corridors, and finally to the side entrance where we were met by Shaneika. We hustled Asa into the back seat while I got in the passenger's side.

"Let's go, Shaneika," Asa said.

Shaneika drove carefully out of the hospital's parking lot to the main downtown artery.

As we were waiting at a stoplight, I threatened, "If you open your wound, Asa, you're going right back in the hospital. And another thing, I'm not paying for this hospital stay. You got that. Not a penny!"

"I'll take responsibility," Asa reassured me.

"You both want to explain to me what happened the other night?"

Shaneika and Asa said in unison, "NO!"

Angry at them, I huffed, "I hope it had something to do with the murder of Juan Gomez and not that stupid horse."

"That colt is the stuff that dreams are made of," Shaneika protested.

"Shaneika, I'm surprised at you. That poor man died because of your colt. You should be doing everything you can to help the police. I'm ashamed of you both. Really I am. Juan had a family who will miss him. He had grandchildren who loved him."

Shaneika narrowed her eyes. "I take umbrage with that, Josiah. The pathway to finding Juan's killer was to find the colt first. Without knowing who took the horse, we were working in the dark."

"Okay. So tell me who stole Last Chance?"

"The less you know—the better," Shaneika said.

"Asa?"

"We can't tell you, Mom. It would make you an accessory-after-the fact. Leave this to us. We'll get it straightened out."

"You'd better. Both of you."

We drove in silence on the way to the Butterfly. I

had no idea if Asa would stay with me or take off. The ride was unsettling. It took us thirty-five minutes to get home. As we drove past the Big House, media trucks almost blocked the way, giving us a few inches of each side of the road to pass by. Reporters clamored on our car, shoving microphones at us, and yelling questions.

I gawked at the number of reporters camping outside the Big House, which sat closer to the road than did the Butterfly. Lady Elsmere's property adjoined to mine and then I recently purchased a farm on the other side of me.

Asa slid down in the car and covered her face with her hands as we barely made it through my electronic gate. We drove slowly up my gravel driveway until Shaneika stopped at the front door of the Butterfly. You couldn't see my house from the road.

I hadn't said a word to either woman after seeing the media camped out on Lady Elsmere's doorsteps, but I just couldn't resist having the final word. "I guess I'll find out what happened in tonight's news."

Shaneika gave me a cheeky grin. Asa just groaned.

So much for keeping things quiet.

20

I watched the local six o'clock news. The anchor stated that Logan Kilkorn was accusing Lady Elsmere of stealing one of his foals, and he would be suing her for ten million dollars. It showed a clip of Logan accusing Lady Elsmere of trespassing and taking one of his foals by force. Another clip showed Lady Elsmere on the portico of the Big House denying the accusations, saying Last Chance had been recovered, but did not address the circumstances of the horse's return.

I turned off the TV after watching the report again on an affiliate news channel. The story was going national. Hopefully, it would blow over in a few weeks. It was obvious Asa found Last Chance on Kilkorn's property.

I wondered if Logan Kilkorn was serious or was just blowing smoke because he got caught with his pants down. It seemed a foolish thing to do, but then I thought Logan Kilkorn was a foolish man. Since the media had broken the story, I could ask questions now, so I decided it was time to get Baby. Asa was sleeping comfortably in her room, Shaneika went back to her office, and the police hadn't shown up at my doorstep with a warrant. Maybe we could get through this without a lot of hoopla.

I left Asa a note and crept out of the house. I needed to check on my bees, so I went through my bee yard. The captured swarm was doing very nicely in its new hive box and the buzzing of the bees sounded pleasant. When the hives are functioning normally, they have a particular hum. And best of all, I didn't see any unusual discharge on the front of the entrances, which meant all the hives seemed in good health. Satisfied, I handed out some apples to some wandering sheep, my mama llama that spat at me after she ate the apple, and Morning Glory who moseyed up to the fence.

"I thought you weren't speaking to me," I said, scratching her ears. Glory shook her head and took the apple. "That's all I've got. Cleaned out."

Seeing there were no more apples, Glory ambled away to munch on grass.

"You're terrible. An ungrateful nag," I yelled.

My American Paint Horse didn't even flick her ear as my insults fell on deaf ears.

Seeing I was being ignored, I went through the gate that connected Lady Elsmere's property with mine. My left leg was already getting tired causing me to wish I had brought a cane or driven my golf cart. You remember I fell off a cliff, don't you?

I opened the back door to the kitchen of the Big House or, at least, I tried. It was locked! Never in the years that Lady Elsmere had owned the Big House has the back door to the kitchen been locked except after 7pm. I knocked and cupped my hands to peer through the glass in the door. I saw Bess wipe her hands on an apron and trot over to unlock the door. I asked, "What gives?"

Bess looked troubled. "We are locked up tighter than a whiskey barrel."

"Because of Last Chance?"

Bess threw herself in a chair and moaned, "You just don't know. You just don't know."

I sat beside her, concerned as I had never seen Bess without a cheerful smile on her face, even when exasperated. "Did Baby do something?" I looked around for my dog. He must have heard my voice because I heard the huge English Mastiff pad down the grand staircase. He came into the kitchen with his nails clicking on the kitchen floor. Happy to see me, Baby rushed over with his tail wagging fiercely. I had to grab it to keep it from swatting me as his tail could really pack a wallop.

Bess got up and put some roast beef in his bowl. The only way we could talk was if Baby was distracted. He gave me an apologetic look before he lumbered over to the food and water bowls that Bess kept for him. I knew food came first with my dog, so I didn't take it personally.

Bess got a bottle of bourbon from a shelf and two shot glasses. She poured the golden liquid in both and handed a glass to me. She drank hers in one gulp.

I was astonished. I had never seen Bess this unnerved before. "Bess, what is it? Maybe I can help."

"Lady Elsmere, my daddy, and this farm are in big trouble. We may lose it all before it is all over."

"Are you talking about Kilkorn's threats? He's a big bag of wind. Lady Elsmere should sue him for libel."

Bess poured herself another drink. "If we go to court, Lady Elsmere will lose."

Sitting back in my chair, I said, "What? You jest."

Bess leaned closer to me. "That colt Lady Elsmere brought home?"

"Yeah?"

"It has the wrong chip in it and the incorrect tattoo number on its lip."

"So, Kilkorn put another chip in the foal and fixed the tattoo number."

Bess poured herself another drink.

I slowly moved the bottle away from her. "What else?"

"Mike doesn't think the foal is Last Chance. He says the foal acts differently than Last Chance, and it's why Jean Harlow rejected him."

"I didn't know Jean Harlow rejected him."

"She did."

"Is this foal doing okay? I mean it isn't dead or anything like that?"

"Mike put it with a surrogate dam. He has a round-the-clock groom checking on him."

"Put this in perspective for me. Are you saying Logan Kilkorn may be right?"

Bess faintly said, "Yes. Lady Elsmere's reputation will be destroyed, not to mention that people may go to prison for this."

"Is there any way to be sure?"

"The vet can order a DNA test, but we all want to find Last Chance, make amends to Kilkorn, and find our foal before this all goes public."

"It has already gone public. Haven't you seen the news and the reporters outside your house?"

"No charges have been filed yet. As long as the police are not involved, we have time to discover the truth and find our horse."

"Here I was thinking Kilkorn was making idle threats." I stood up abruptly causing Baby to glance at me with water dripping from his mouth folds. "I'm going to find Mike."

"He's in Barn #3."

"Tell Lady Elsmere that I'll be back. Maybe tomorrow."

"I'll tell her you were here, Josiah."

"Thanks, Bess. Baby, come."

My Mastiff followed as he had finished eating and was ready for an adventure. Sleeping next to Lady Elsmere was not his idea of a fun night. Besides he missed his Kitty Kaboodle, a stray litter of cats that were Baby's pets.

I couldn't walk anymore as my left leg was throbbing, so I borrowed one of the farm's golf carts and was off to see Mike.

21

The barn doors were closed and a guard stood on either end of the barn. "Hey, is Mike in there?" I asked.

"Maybe," the guard said.

Since I was not familiar with this security guard and noticed he was wearing a gun, I asked very politely, "Can you tell him Josiah needs to speak with him, please?"

"Maybe," the guard replied in a surly tone.

"Like right now."

Baby stood up and growled.

The guard stepped back to the barn doors, slid one over, and yelled into it. "Mr. Connor? Some lady by the name of Josiah wishes to speak with you."

I heard Mike yell back to let me in.

The guard said, "You can go in."

"I have a physical ailment. Will you open the door so I can drive the golf cart in?"

The guard looked at me with great distrust.

"Look, I'm old and frail. I'm not gonna steal any

horse. I live next door."

The guard raised his thick eyebrows in need of a trim. They looked like two caterpillars mating on top of each eye. "Ah, you're the kooky bee lady. Heard about you."

"Gee, thanks. Can you please open the door?"

The guard tilted his head, sizing up Baby who was still softly growling. "He's a big one."

"He also attacks on command," I lied, knowing that Baby never did anything on command except eat.

The guard chuckled. "I don't think so. I have one of these at home. He won't attack unless you are really threatened."

I always soften toward anyone who is fond of Mastiffs, so I pleaded, "From one Mastiff owner to another, please open the door."

"Sure thing." The guard went up to Baby and slipped him a dried piece of jerky from a pouch tucked in his pocket. Of course, Baby gobbled it and allowed himself to be petted by the man.

I gave Baby a curt glance as the guard slid open one of the barn's massive doors. "You know, Baby, one of these days I'm going to trade you in for a Rottweiler."

Baby slurped and licked me with his sticky tongue. I sighed. What can I tell you? I loved this messy, droopy dog.

Once the door was opened I drove the cart inside. The guard immediately closed the barn door causing the barn to become very dark. The only light filtering in was through the windows in the stalls. I stopped the golf cart and called out Mike's name. Of course, it was hard to hear with the fans on. "Mike. MIKE!"

Mike popped his head out from a stall at the far end of the barn. "Here, Josiah."

I waved and drove my cart very slowly down the barn aisle looking into each stall as I passed. Most of the stalls were empty with just a few mares and foals residing. I stopped ten feet from where Mike was mucking out a stall. Surprised that he was doing such menial work, I asked, "Where are your helpers?"

"Charles and I are not letting anyone come in this barn and have access to Last Chance."

"You mean you don't want anyone coming in and seeing a colt that is not Last Chance and possibly testify against you."

"Ah, crap. Who told you?"

"Bess. She's very worried. I would imagine the entire family is worried. Their future is tied up with Lady Elsmere. If she goes down, so do they."

"And me as well."

"The only reason you let me in is because I had never seen the colt. I can't testify one way or the other about the identity of the baby."

Mike gave a quick nod. He laid the pitchfork against the barn wall.

"What are you going to do?"

Mike answered, "I don't know, Josiah. I've been racking my brain, trying to figure out what happened."

"It's as plain as the nose on your face. It was a setup to frame Lady Elsmere."

"You expect me to believe a man was killed to get revenge on Lady Elsmere? Even I don't think Logan J. Kilkorn would go that far. He's a bit shady, but murder? I don't know."

I looked in a stall where a grey mare was nursing a black foal, which had the white star on the forehead accompanied by four white stocking feet. "Is this the foal?"

Mike leaned up against a stall door, peering through the bars in the door. "Yep, that's him. He's the right age, sex, has the correct markings, but the tattoo number is off and the chip gives Logan's owner information."

"And there's the fact that Jean Harlow rejected him."

"Yeah, there's that." Mike took a bandanna out of his pocket and wiped the sweat off his face.

"Tell me what happened, Mike. Walk me through it."

"We really thought Logan had stolen the colt. He's been making threats that he was going to take Lady Elsmere down. Horses are nothing more than money to him. He doesn't care what happens to them after he's used them up, and we both know that he will go to illegal lengths to win."

"Thus drugging a competitor's horse."

"Precisely, Josiah. This is why owners guard their horses before races."

"If Lady Elsmere got her reforms, that would cost him money on animals he didn't prize. His ban will be lifted in a year; thus the urgency to shut her down."

"How did Logan have access to the competitor's horse?"

"It was very easy. His groom was friends with the competitor's groom. They visited and Logan's man just slipped something nasty in the horse's water when his friend had his back turned. An hour later, the horse was ill."

"And you're sure it was done on orders from Logan Kilkorn."

"The Racing Commission believed so, even though Logan denied it. Said he knew nothing about it."

"Enough about Logan Kilkorn. What was Asa's part in all of this?"

"To get on Logan's property to search for our colt."

"She trespassed?"

Mike looked sheepish. "Not really. She arranged to meet Logan's son, Micah, and got onto the property through him."

I didn't like the way Mike was speaking of how Asa got on to the Kilkorn's property. I felt he was leaving something out, but I didn't interrupt.

"Lady Elsmere borrowed a road-front field from a buddy of hers, who owed her a favor. The buddy's farm was not a mile from the Kilkorn farm. In case Asa found the colt, she and her men were to remove the colt and bring him to our camp where we waited with a vet and Jean Harlow. Asa found a colt in a root cellar and brought him to us."

"Why does Kilkorn think Lady Elsmere is behind the taking of this colt?"

"Asa had to bust through Kilkorn's fences to get away and several of Kilkorn's men gave chase. They passed the field where we were waiting and recognized us."

"But Logan Kilkorn didn't call the police," I pointed out. "I think that is rather telling."

"We didn't call the police either."

"I know horse people like to handle disputes themselves. Airing dirty laundry in public is almost unheard of. Gives racing a bad name."

"Precisely," Mike agreed.

"What's the next step in this fight?"

"Wait for the DNA report. If this colt is really from Kilkorn's stables, we'll return the colt on the down-low and quietly make restitution. Lady Elsmere will have to write a big, fat check after Kilkorn signs a non-disclosure agreement. The lawyers will make it happen."

"What about Last Chance?"

"Personally, I think the colt is dead."

I said, "I hope that is not true, but one thing is for sure—Logan Kilkorn is up to his eyeballs in this mess. No one puts an expensive Thoroughbred colt in a root cellar unless it is for a nefarious purpose."

"We only have Asa's word that is where she found the colt."

"Are you saying my daughter is lying?"

"No, I'm saying if this goes to court, we only have Asa's testimony that the colt was found in a root cellar. Kilkorn will state she took the colt from the nursery barn."

I stepped closer to Mike and hissed, "Get this straight. Asa's not going to testify in court about anything. She was never here. Got that?"

"Sure, Josiah." Mike was a little stunned at my ferocity, so he backed off. "How's Asa?" he asked, softening his tone. "I plan on visiting her in the hospital later this afternoon."

"Don't bother. Asa is incommunicado"

"What does that mean?"

"It means she's out of anyone's reach for the moment. See you around, Mike." I motioned for Mike to open the barn door for me, which he did. I floored the electric cart and sped out quickly almost running Mike down because I was mad. So mad.

It looked like I was going to have to find that darn colt myself.

22

I have a bad temper. Goes with the red hair. I took Baby home to keep an eye on Asa. She was still sleeping. Good. It was time to have a showdown with Lady Elsmere, so I sped back up to the Big House, my second visit today.

Lady Elsmere was holed up in her bedroom like some pasha. We had a lengthy and somewhat testy discussion before I yelled, "So that's just it! You're giving up looking for Last Chance? And what about poor Juan? Find out who took the colt and you'll likely find his killer."

She put her tea cup down on her pink satin bedspread. "I realize that, Josiah. I can't sleep nights thinking about Juan's wife and family. It's just that we don't know where to look. We've run out of leads," she said this barely looking me in the eye. "I can tell you're angry."

"You think? I didn't want to get Asa involved and against my better judgment, I called her. Now look what's happened. She ended up in the hospital, and she might go to jail over this horse."

"I know. I know. I feel terrible, but I didn't know she would be injured and might be prosecuted."

"I'm just glad they don't hang horse thieves anymore. You got her into this mess, June. Now you get her out," I demanded.

Lady Elsmere's eyes glistened with tears.

Oh, no. Lady Elsmere's ultimate weapon. "June, don't you dare cry. I mean it."

"Josiah, I'm so sorry. I didn't mean for all this to happen. A stolen horse, a dead employee, my farm in jeopardy, and Asa hurt. I know it's my fault."

I went through a dresser and found several handkerchiefs. I gave Lady Elsmere one decorated with hollyhock leaves and berries. It was a handkerchief I had embroidered for Lady Elsmere years ago. "Can't you pay that leech off and make this go away?"

"My lawyers are working on it. They've been in constant contact with Kilkorn. I'm doing all I can. Let's change the subject please. How is Asa?"

"Fair to middling. She won't be participating in any dance marathons for a while."

"I'll go to the hospital today and visit. I'll make arrangements for all her medical bills."

"You do that," I said curtly. No, I wasn't going to tell Lady Elsmere that Asa was sleeping next door. Let the old woman experience a little anxiety for a change.

Yes, I know it was mean, but I didn't care.

I left in a huff, leaving Lady Elsmere in a crying jag of tears, calling after me.

I shouldn't have left like that, but I was determined to discover who took the colt, so we could find who killed Juan Gomez. I was too busy on the hunt for clues, so it would be sometime later when I felt the pangs of remorse.

23

I huffed and puffed my way to the maintenance barn. That's where all the equipment like tractors, hay bailers, trucks, and more were stored and worked on when malfunctioning. Most of the farm vehicles were over forty years old, but kept in tiptop shape by one master mechanic and assistants. The ancient equipment was superior to those newly-made machines available on the market, and Lady Elsmere's people could fix anything that had wheels. Besides working on Lady Elsmere's equipment, they also worked on neighbors' machinery. They were allowed to use Lady Elsmere's maintenance barn and equipment. The only conditions were that they pay for anything broken or lost tools, oil, and gas. Worked well for everyone involved.

I poked my head inside one of the bays, which smelled of human sweat, grease and spilled petrol. "Hey, is Renata around?"

"She's around back taking a break, Mrs. Reynolds."

"Thank you, Jose."

Jose waved his wrench and went back to changing the oil on a neighbor's car.

I drove the golf cart to the back of the building and spotted Renata sitting at a picnic table gobbling a pupusa de pollo. I got out and sat opposite her.

Renata looked surprised and put down her food. She was petite with brown hair and dark, expressive eyes that didn't miss much. "Mrs. Reynolds, what are you doing here? I thought no visitors were allowed for the time being."

"Do you know why?"

Renata shook her head, causing her long ponytail to sway. "Things have been pretty tense around here for the past several days. I assume it has to do with Last Chance, but why the sudden lockdown since yesterday I couldn't fathom." She gave me a cheeky grin. "Want to enlighten me? I know *you* know."

This young woman and I go back a few years. She was an upstart twenty-year-old who boasted she could restore my antiquated Volkswagen bus. I let her have at it, thinking she would fail, but to my surprise Renata succeeded in bringing that old, rusty bus back to life. She painted it turquoise and restored the upholstery to its original color. I must say my bus purrs like a kitten, and now I don't let anyone touch it but Renata.

I replied, "I was hoping you could enlighten me."

"What about?"

"Juan Gomez. Did you know him?"

"Well enough to say hello and chat for a few minutes. I never socialized with him."

"Never had a beer with him? Nothing like that?"

"Yeah, he would come by and shoot the bull with the boys before his shift. Maybe have a beer or two."

"I thought Lady Elsmere didn't allow drinking on the job."

Renata gave me another grin. "What Lady Elsmere doesn't know won't hurt her. We keep a cooler in the shop. Sometimes a person needs a cold beer on a hot summer's afternoon during their break. Nobody gets drunk. Doesn't affect our work. You're not gonna tell on us, are you?"

"Not if I get a cold beer every now and then."

"I knew you were a good egg."

"Let's get back to Juan. What do you know about him?"

"He was planning on retiring soon. Juan had arthritis, and it was getting harder and harder for him to work."

"Any other medical problems?"

"Not that I'm aware of."

"Besides arthritis, what was going on in Juan's life?"

"He was having problems with his wife, Valeria. They were estranged."

"Why?"

"I think Juan liked to gamble—play the ponies. From what I understand, it caused the couple financial distress, so she left him—or she kicked him out. I don't know which."

"Juan was in his sixties. Was this gambling recent or a lifelong issue?"

"I don't know. He would talk to the guys in the shop, and I would listen as I worked. He was a loud talker. I would hear snatches of the conversations from the bull pen." Renata gave me a sly smile.

I hid my amusement that Renata was a snoop like I was. It's amazing what one can learn by carefully eavesdropping. I asked, "Was he especially close to anyone who worked on the farm?"

"Not really. Juan was closer to us because we are Hispanic like he was."

"Was Juan American born in the States or an immigrant?"

"I think he came over the border as a small child. He said he was originally from Mexico, but doesn't remember the village."

"What about family besides his wife?"

"I think he had grandchildren."

"Is there anyone working today I can ask?"

"Please don't, Mrs. Reynolds. The Hispanics who work here will either not speak with you about Juan or make something up. We take care of our own."

"Why are you speaking with me then?"

"I didn't care for Juan." Renata took a swig of her soft drink.

That statement caught me by surprise. "Oh, why?"

"Juan was a typical man from his generation. He kept telling me that a real woman needs to be married, have children—that kind of thing. He would do this right in front of my male co-workers. The sermonizing got old. Juan made things rougher for me working here with the men because of his attitude. He stirred them up against me."

"What do you think happened the night he died?"

"I think Juan opened the gates for the intruders."

"Tell me your version of events, Renata."

"It's very simple. I suspect Juan must have needed money and made some sort of deal with the kidnappers, opened the gate for them, and then got shot for his troubles. Listen, remember the dead guy you found in the corn maze last year at Lady Elsmere's Halloween party?"

"How could I forget?"

"Since that incident, this farm has been locked up tighter than Fort Knox. There is no way those kidnappers got in without help from the inside."

"What about other employees who work the night shift?"

"They don't matter. It was Juan's car discovered next to the nursery barn. He had to be in on it as he was sitting in his car having a candy bar. That tells me his guard was down. He figured they would take the horse and leave as quickly as possible. There's also the fact that his gun was still in its holster. If he was trying to prevent the theft, he would have gotten out of his car with the gun drawn. He was in on it all right."

"Anything else?"

Renata paused. "I don't think so. If I think of anything else, I'll let you know."

"Renata, will you get chastised for speaking with me?"

"I'll tell the boys that you want the VW bus looked at. They'll believe me."

"Okay. Tell me one more thing. Do you know where Valeria Gomez lives?"

"Cardinal Valley subdivision on the west side of town. Little Mexico."

"Thanks, Renata."

"Take care, Mrs. Reynolds. If Juan wasn't in on the scam, then someone else who works here was. Someone had to open the gates. Be careful. I know how you like to poke around."

"I'll be careful. Promise." I got into the golf cart and headed back home, wondering if I could visit Valeria Gomez before Asa woke up.

I decided to wait. I didn't trust Asa to stay at the Butterfly if I left her alone for an extended period of time. I just couldn't take the chance of Asa absconding if given the opportunity. She could end up anywhere on the globe in a matter of hours.

This made me feel sad. It's certainly not the mother-daughter relationship I craved.

I loved Asa, but I can't say I liked her—at the moment.

24

I found Charles at the practice track watching horses being put through their paces.

He didn't seem surprised to see me.

I rested my arms on the railing as he did and watched the practice race with several horses. "Are they yours?"

Charles answered, "No, they are owned by a Middle Eastern sheik. See that man on the other side of the track with a stopwatch."

I looked across the track and noticed a man in a green shirt and khaki pants.

"That's the sheik's trainer. I'm sure by the end of the week, he'll move the sheik's horses to another horse farm due to all this negative attention by the press. One thing Middle Eastern potentates dislike is drama," Charles said, waving away an insect.

"Are the reporters still outside?"

"Yeah. The neighbors are raising hell because the reporters are blocking the road with their vans."

"Do you blame them?"

"No. You missed the helicopter flying overhead. Scared the horses so much, we had to bring them in from the pastures."

"Charles, can you answer some questions for me?"

"You sure you want to involve yourself in this?"

"I'm not interested in Last Chance per say. I want to ask about Juan Gomez."

Charles ruminated, "In all the hubbub, everyone seems to have forgotten about poor Juan."

I asked, "What do the police say?"

"They are telling us nothing."

"Do they think it is an inside job?"

Charles nodded.

"Do they think it was Juan?"

"I'm not sure they do. Mike, my entire family, Miss Shaneika, and the employees working that night have taken lie detector tests. I get the drift from Detective Drake's questions he thinks someone other than Juan opened the gates."

"What about the surveillance tapes?"

"Everything had been wiped clean."

"How is that possible?"

"That's what the police want to know."

"Isn't there a backup system like in the cloud or something similar?"

"Not there either."

"Don't you have a backup system?"

"We have two, but both were wiped clean."

"Are you a suspect, Charles?"

"They are breathing down my neck, Josiah. I think there is a distinct possibility they might arrest me. I'm at the top of their list. I take care of the security monitors and the backup systems. The only reason I haven't been arrested so far is that my lie detector test was clean."

"That's poppycock. What reason would you have to steal Last Chance?"

"That's the other reason I haven't been arrested, Josiah. I lack motive. Nevertheless, the police are building a case against me. I'm sure of it."

I didn't reply. I felt Charles was being paranoid, but then again maybe he was correct. Charles, like most African-American men, grow anxious when the police look at him more than once. I understood his trepidation. "Do you think someone on the inside did this?"

"I think it was either Mike, Juan, or one of the other guards."

I was surprised he mentioned Mike. They had worked closely together for years. "What can you tell me about Juan?"

"He toiled for Lady Elsmere a long time, came to work on time, rarely complained. I thought he was a good employee."

"What about his family?"

"I don't know anything except that he was married

and sometimes brought his grandchildren to see the horses when we had an open house."

"If he had grandchildren, he had children. Know anything about them?"

Charles hesitated before answering. I could tell he was growing tired. The strain of the past several days played on his face.

"I'm sorry, Charles. I don't mean to badger you, but you know I'm good at solving puzzles."

"Don't apologize, Josiah. I'm just worn out with worry. I know you are trying to help."

I put my hand on his arm, giving a squeeze. "Can you tell me where he lived?"

"Sure."

"And where his wife lives?"

"What do you mean?"

"They were separated."

Charles looked surprised. "Let me ask Bess." He plucked out his phone and called Bess asking her to go into his office off the kitchen. "Give Bess a second. She has to boot up the computer." A minute later, Charles gave me two addresses.

"I'm going to check these out."

"Suit yourself, Josiah, but be careful. We don't know who is involved, and they might not like you sticking your nose in this affair."

"One more thing."

"Yeah."

"Is the foal Asa found Last Chance?"

Charles answered sadly, "I knew the moment Jean Harlow rejected that foal, he was not Last Chance. We have made a terrible mistake. Lady Elsmere and her estate are in big, big trouble. I don't see our way out of this. Logan J. Kilkorn could bankrupt Lady Elsmere or take away her farm in a settlement."

"That's what Mike said."

"Mike is right."

I took my leave, so glad I was not in the hot seat this time. However I couldn't sit idly by and let someone take Lady Elsmere's farm away from her. I was angry with the old biddy, but that was temporary. I also had to fix it so Asa was never mentioned to the authorities. Oh, gosh, I was starting to feel the anxiety Charles felt.

I guess misery loves company.

25

I pulled into a driveway on Londonderry Drive in the Cardinal Valley subdivision and took in the house before me. It was a standard red brick house built in the sixties with a large picture window. I knew it would contain three bedrooms and one bathroom, a nice-sized backyard with a metal fence. I know this because I lived in Cardinal Valley when Brannon and I first married. I made a mental note to visit our first house when I left here, but now was not the time to go down memory lane.

The yard was freshly mowed, and whoever lived here loved flowers with splashy bold colors—white snapdragons, Mexican sunflowers, orange trumpet vines, yellow black-eyed susans, purple morning glories, and brilliant zinnias. The windows showed no sign of dust and the brass mailbox near the front door was still shiny from its last polishing. The owner of this house took pride in its ownership and obviously loved it.

There were two pickup trucks in the driveway, so I

knew someone was home. I knocked on the front door and waited. Finally a woman in her sixties opened the door and peered out. Her graying hair was pulled back into a bun and she wore a cotton house dress with a daisy pattern. The woman looked exhausted, and her eyes were red from crying. "Yes?"

"Mrs. Gomez?"

"Madre de Dios! I hope you are not selling something. There has been a death in the family. Leave us be." She started to close the door.

"No, Mrs. Gomez. I'm not selling anything, but I need to speak with you."

She gave me a closer look. "Are you from the police?"

"No, ma'am. I'm Mrs. Reynolds. I live next door to Lady Elsmere. I discovered your husband."

"Why are you here?" She eyed me suspiciously.

"To pay my respects and tell you what happened. I would want to know if I were in your shoes."

Mrs. Gomez blinked a few times, then opened the door to let me in. The inside of the house was just as colorful and cheerful as the outside. Bright oranges and yellows accented by splashes of red dominated the house. However, the colorful palette was dulled by the grief of Mrs. Gomez. Through the back sliding door, I could see two adult men with their wives and children sitting on the back patio eating.

"I'm sorry. I see you have your family gathered.

What I have to say won't take long."

"No, please, sit down." She beckoned to a chair. "You said you found my husband."

I sat down and put my purse on the floor. Mrs. Gomez sat in the opposite chair.

"I was with Miss Todd when it was discovered that Last Chance was missing."

Mrs. Gomez muttered something under her breath in Spanish. I caught the word diablo. I'm sure she was referring to the horse and not Shaneika Mary Todd. At least, I hope she was.

I waited for Mrs. Gomez to continue and when she didn't, I spoke, "When we couldn't find the colt, we went outside and saw that your husband's car was parked near the barn. We went up to it and saw him sitting in the driver's seat. I knocked on the window and when he didn't respond, I opened the door. It was then we discovered that Mr. Gomez had passed."

Mrs. Gomez rubbed her eyes and reached for a box of tissues on the coffee table. I handed the box to her.

"Did my husband seem to have been in pain at the time of his death?"

"We thought he was taking a nap, so no, Mrs. Gomez. I think his death was quick."

"Wasn't there much blood in the car? How can a man be shot and there not be blood everywhere in the car? Wouldn't you have noticed that something was not right?"

I was stumped. Neither Shaneika nor I noticed blood splatter on the windows of the car. "I don't know what to tell you, Mrs. Gomez, but we didn't observe anything untoward in the car. We didn't know Juan had been shot until we tried to help him." There was no need to tell her that he thudded carelessly to the ground after we opened the car door, so I didn't.

"It was nice you tried to help my husband. I thank you."

Seeing that Mrs. Gomez was ready to end the conversation and show me the door, I asked, "May I have a glass of water, please?"

"Of course." Mrs. Gomez rose to go into the kitchen and I followed her.

"I didn't see Mr. Gomez's Toyota outside."

"The police haven't discharged it yet."

"Is there a date for the funeral?"

Mrs. Gomez clutched the side of the kitchen counter.

"Mrs. Gomez, are you all right?"

"It's nothing. All this stress makes me dizzy. The medical examiner won't release the body for another week or so. She says she is waiting on a toxicology report before my Juan is let go. It distresses me so to think of him lying on a cold slab in a morgue." Mrs. Gomez filled a glass with tap water and handed it to me.

"Let's sit down then." I took the glass from her and

went over to the kitchen table. Mrs. Gomez followed, glancing out the glass sliding door. There was a faint smile as she gazed at her grandchildren before turning her attention back to me.

I took a sip of water before asking, "I see your wedding picture on the wall along with your children. That's a beautiful wedding dress you're wearing."

"It was my mother's wedding dress and the lace veil was my grandmother's."

"I suppose the dress and veil were handed down to your daughters."

"I have only two sons. Their wives wanted more modern wedding dresses."

I could tell Mrs. Gomez disapproved. "Perhaps your granddaughters then.

She remarked, "Perhaps."

"Were you married here?"

"Yes, Juan and I met at St. Paul's downtown. It was a church social for singles." Mrs. Gomez chuckled. "It wasn't love at first sight for me, but Juan was determined. I think I dated him from sheer fatigue. He kept asking me out every other day, saying 'what will it take, woman?'"

"How long were you married?"

"It would have been thirty-eight years next month."

"I'm a widow myself."

Mrs. Gomez looked at me with pleading eyes. "Does it get any better?"

"My husband left me and died before we could reconcile. There was much anger associated with his death."

"He left you?"

"For a younger woman. A common story with middle-aged men."

"Juan and I were separated at the time of his death."

"Another woman?"

"Oh, heavens no. He had a sickness. Gambling." Mrs. Gomez inched her chair closer to mine. "Juan was involved in a car accident two years ago. He got a large settlement. In our culture, a windfall like that is used for the entire family, but Juan started gambling. He had never gambled before, so it was a shock to us all. Before I knew it, he had gambled away most of the money. I hid what was left and begged him to get help, but Juan refused. I gave him an ultimatum—either get help or get out. You know what Juan did, Mrs. Reynolds? He left me. He found where I hid the money, took it, and left me. What do you think of that?"

"I'm very sorry, Mrs. Gomez. Such heartache. Where did he go?"

"To some two-bit rooming house on the north side of town. I went there once with my sons to talk with him—you know, knock some sense into him, but he wouldn't budge. Juan was going to do what he wanted to do 'since he had sacrificed his entire life for us.' It was crazy talk."

"Was that the last time you saw him alive?"

"No, he would come occasionally to eat with the family, wash his clothes, or gather a few of his things. It was so odd. He acted so normally I thought he had come home for good. I'd go to the grocery store or out into my garden, but when I entered the house again, he was gone."

"Do you think he came back looking for money?"

Mrs. Gomez bit her lip. "I think you might be right. He was looking for money. After he started gambling, I hid my personal money, checks, and credit cards. He never found those."

"But he found the settlement money?"

"Unfortunately, I hid it underneath the driver's seat of my car. Not a very imaginative place to hide money, thinking back on it."

"Hindsight is 20-20. Did you ever confront Mr. Gomez when he came home?"

"No, I and my sons acted as though nothing had happened. We thought this might ease his passage back into the family fold. We didn't want to start a fight with him."

"Mrs. Gomez, you said he didn't start gambling until he had this car accident. Do you think it might have something to do with it? I mean, did Mr. Gomez have any injuries?"

"He got quite a nasty bump on his head, a couple of broken ribs, and a fractured femur. A drunk ran through a stop sign and totaled his car. The drunk was severely injured and died several months later. We thought Juan was lucky."

"I just think it odd that the gambling coincided with the accident."

"My feelings were that Juan saw that his life had been in danger, feared death, and wanted a release of some kind. Gambling provided that release. You know, Mrs. Reynolds, life is a thief. For every boon, it takes something away. Fortune granted my husband his life and a large settlement from that accident, but stole his soul. Yes, life is a thief."

How well I knew. How well I knew.

26

I made a beeline to the police station. While I was heading toward Detective Drake's office, I ran into Detective Kelly. Yes, the same Kelly Asa had dumped after high school. "Is Drake in?"

"He's out in the field. Why are you here, Jo?"

"I wanted to ask him something about Juan Gomez's autopsy and to see if he would release my van. This rental car is costing me a fortune."

"Come to my office. I can help you." We entered the elevator and went to the fourth floor where Kelly escorted me to his office.

I looked around the sparse office. "Wow, you've got your own window." I went over and looked out. What greeted me was the wall of the next building. "Better than nothing, I guess."

"I'm a junior detective. I don't get the perks like views."

"At least the furniture is new."

"What can I do you for? You said something about your van."

"I need it. Your forensic boys should have gone over it by now."

Kelly picked up the phone and pressed a number. He asked about my van and then hung up. "It's ready. You can pick it up anytime."

"I assume the police didn't find anything incriminating."

"Naw, but I expect a couple bottles of honey have been nicked."

Still standing, I quipped, "The price of doing business with the police."

Kelly looked embarrassed.

"Oh, don't get your panties in wad. I'm just joking."

"Was there anything else?"

"Yeah, I went to see Mrs. Gomez to pay my respects."

"Sure you did."

"I'll ignore the sarcasm in your voice, Kelly. She told me that Juan had a gambling problem. Maybe he owed money and made a deal with someone to open the gate."

Kelly didn't respond.

"Oh, so you guys are thinking along the same line."

"No comment."

"Ah, huh. Has the autopsy report come in yet?" I asked.

"No comment."

"Mrs. Gomez told me her husband had this gambling problem since he had a car accident several years back. Before then he was clean—not addicted. Don't you find that interesting?"

Kelly said, "I'm listening."

"I would certainly look for any brain lesions or tumors which might have affected the man's behavior."

"Anything else, Dr. Reynolds?"

I made a face. "Nope. Sarcasm does not become you."

"Well, I have a question. Where's Asa now?"

"I don't know." I hated fibbing to Kelly, but I had to keep Asa's name out of this mess.

"We heard though an informant that Micah Kilkorn fell ill at the Chevy Chase Inn after he ate chili with a strange dark-haired woman. The bartender had never seen her before. The description sounded a lot like Asa."

I reiterated, "There are a lot of women who look like Asa. This is a college town, after all, with many beauties."

Kelly stood behind his desk, giving me that inquisitive look he always did when questioning something. I don't think he believed me. Maybe I was trying to sell it too hard.

"Anything else, Kelly?"

"I guess not."

"Listen."

"Yeah?" He sat down and rummaged through some files.

"I want to drive my van home. Can I leave the rental here and you hand the fob over. I'll call the car rental and tell them to pick their car up here and get the fob from you."

Kelly looked up from his desk. "Okay. But they need to pick the car up within two hours. I have to get the kids from school today."

"You're a life saver. Thanks a bunch." I left Kelly's office feeling better than when I rose this morning. I loved finding out secrets. They really made my day.

27

I hurried home in my VW van. I had been gone most of the day when I expected to be absent for only a few hours. I wondered if Asa was going to be home when I got back. I never could tell with that kid.

Baby met me at the front door with his tail wagging, which cheered me. I smiled hearing the refrigerator door slam shut in the kitchen.

"Asa, you're up?" I called out, entering the kitchen.

Asa was in her hospital gown with a sheet draped about her hips and dragging on the floor. "Where were you?"

"I left a note."

"Did you?"

"I went to get my van. What are you rooting for?"

"I'm hungry. I want something to eat."

"That's a good sign. I have a nice leek soup in the freezer. It will be gentle to your stomach."

"Yuck!"

"It's a really good soup, and I can toast some garlic

bread to go along with it. Maybe you would prefer a bone broth."

Asa pouted, just like she did when a kid. "That doesn't sound too bad. Got anything sweet?"

"I can rustle up some chocolate cake or homemade strawberry ice cream."

"I'll take the ice cream while the soup is heating."

"Sounds like a fair trade. I'll get it for you right now. Sit down before you bust something open."

Asa sat at my Nakashima dining table. "Can you change my dressing after I eat?"

I teased, "Hmm, what yummy conversation for a meal. Sure, I can change your weeping funky dressing for a clean one later."

Asa gave a bitter smirk. "You just gotta stick that knife in and twist it, don't ya?"

"What do you think mothers are for, Asa? We love to torment our children."

Asa blew me a raspberry while I spooned a bowl of strawberry ice cream. I let it soften on the kitchen island while heating her soup and toasting the bread.

"Here you go," I said, placing the ice cream before her. "The soup will be ready in a moment."

Asa dove into the ice cream with relish. "Nobody makes homemade ice cream like you, Mom."

"This weekend will be the last for the peaches. I can make you some peach ice cream."

"I don't know if I'll be here then. I think I need to leave town."

"That may be wise, but not for a while. You need to heal."

"Heard any whispering about me?"

"I ran into Kelly at the police station. He said there was a rumor that Micah Kilkorn got ill after eating chili with a brunette woman."

Asa put down her spoon. "It's only a matter of time before Kelly shows Micah my photo."

"Why? Neither Micah nor Logan Kilkorn have filed a report yet. You know how the police like listening to gossip. It's how they pick up tips, but until a report is filed, the police are not going to ask about you or anyone else. They have too much to do rather than chase phantom crimes."

"Kelly will. You know he will."

I sighed. "You're probably right. Wait a couple of days until you feel better and then get out of town."

"I'll rest today and then leave tomorrow afternoon."

Why did Asa never listen to me? I guess all daughters are like that with their mothers. "Are you sure resting today is enough to get you back on your feet?"

"I'll make do, Mom. Like always."

"I fear for you, Asa. You are taking too many risks."

"I always play it safe."

"Really? I don't think so. I saw your body after they brought you back in from surgery. You have scars everywhere, and the doctor told me they found a metal fragment in your wound. Now that sounds like a bullet."

"She wasn't supposed to tell you my medical issues."

"Well, she did, little missy. You're not denying it, I see."

Asa remained silent.

"You make me so mad. Who are you, Asa? What are you? Who do you really work for?"

"I am an art insurance investigator."

"You're full of crap, is what you are. Be that way, Asa. You make me so angry."

"You've said that you're mad twice now. I get that you are angry, Mom. I really do."

There was nothing more to say. I got her soup with garlic bread, and another bowl of strawberry ice cream. After eating, Asa went back to bed.

I remained up half the night worrying about what was to become of my daughter.

28

I answered the front door to discover Shaneika Mary Todd looking distraught. "Is Asa here?"

"No, she's not," I lied.

"It's okay, Mom. Let her in." I turned around to see Asa still in her hospital gown standing in the hallway.

I opened the door wider for Shaneika. "Why do I even bother to protect you?"

"I'm sorry, Josiah, but I need to speak with Asa. I went to the hospital but they said Asa had checked out."

Asa replied, "That's a nice way of explaining it. I went against doctor's orders and left." She went over to the couch and sat down. "What's going on?"

Shaneika and I followed Asa into the great room.

"Do you think that wise, Asa?" Shaneika said, her forehead creasing.

"That's what I've been telling her, but she won't listen," I complained.

Asa waved my concerns away. "What did you need, Shaneika?"

"I just wanted to tell you the DNA report came back. The foal you captured from Logan Kilkorn is not Last Chance."

"Jumping Jehoshaphat! The manure is going to hit the fan now," I said.

Asa seemed startled upon reflecting on Shaneika's news. Shaneika and I gathered about while Asa thought this news through. She finally said, "We've all been played. The kidnapping was a setup from the start. It was planned to bring Lady Elsmere to her knees—to stop her racing reform activism."

Shaneika suggested, "I think you should leave town, Asa. Let Lady Elsmere handle this."

"What about Last Chance?" Asa asked.

Shaneika threw her hands up. "I think the horse is dead. There is no other explanation of why we can't find him. This thing is getting too murky. I don't want to see you hurt further. I'm not sure why you passed out bleeding, but I don't want to be the cause of you getting injured. I'll just have to accept that colt is gone. We'll try again to mate Jean Harlow with Comanche."

I kept quiet not mentioning that Kilkorn might take Comanche or Jean Harlow as part of the settlement with Lady Elsmere. Instead, I glanced at Asa. "I think Shaneika is giving you good advice. Take it."

Asa replied, "I still think the colt is at Kilkorn's estate. From what I've learned about the man, I don't think he would put a colt down."

Shaneika said, "Did you not learn that he is banned from racing because he tried to dope someone else's horse? Horses are just money to the man. He doesn't care about them." She leaned in closer to Asa. "Lady Elsmere and I have talked it over. You're to leave town. We will post money in your account when things have cooled down."

Asa protested, "Do neither of you find it strange that Kilkorn has not filed a report with the police? He just has made public accusations. Very odd to say the least."

"You don't know that, Asa. He and his son might have had breakfast this morning comparing notes and are on their way to the police station right now. Or a complaint is sitting on some officer's desk waiting for further investigation," I argued.

"There is nothing to tie me in with either Logan or Micah Kilkorn."

There was no reasoning with Asa about this. Like a three-year-old, she had planted her feet firmly and was not about to budge. She surprised both Shaneika and myself when she said, "Don't worry, Shaneika. I agree that I have lived past my usefulness in this scenario. I already decided to leave this afternoon after I make arrangements."

"You need to recuperate. I feel so bad about you getting hurt," Shaneika replied, obviously relieved that Asa was leaving town. It was one less ball in the air.

"It's not your fault," Asa replied, refusing to explain the origin of her injuries.

Shaneika stood. "I've got to get to the office. I just wanted to thank you for everything you did for us, Asa. Please take care."

"It's okay, Shaneika."

"Sure it is, Asa. Everything will be okay."

Asa seemed tired and rested her eyes. "Mom, will you see Shaneika out?"

"Don't bother, Josiah. I know the way." Shaneika shot Asa another glance. "Take care, Asa."

"You too, sister."

I walked Shaneika out and watched her leave. When I closed the door I could hear Asa on the landline making arrangements for her departure. I felt sad—so I called to Baby and we visited my bees.

My bees always made me feel happy.

Asa did not.

29

Asa had a driver pick her up and take her to the airport. She wouldn't let me drive her. I recognized the driver as Cody who had stayed with me after my fall years back. I waved to Cody as he gave a curt nod to me. "Asa, call me when you arrive at your destination."

"I will, Mom."

"Are you going to New York?"

"No, I think somewhere beachy."

"You'll let me know where you are."

"I will. Promise." Asa leaned over and kissed me.

"You look ridiculous," I said, referring to her floppy hat and oversized sunglasses. I glanced at the SUV's dark tinted windows and wondered why Asa thought she needed a disguise.

Asa laughed. "This is just in case there are still reporters camped out on the road."

"I think most of them are gone."

"That's good. Hey, pet Baby goodbye for me. I didn't want to disturb him. He's taking his usual afternoon nap."

"I will."

Cody opened the SUV's door for Asa and loaded her bag in the car. She rolled down the tinted window. "Take care, Mother. I'll call as soon as I get settled."

"As soon as you land, Asa. Don't make me worry."

"I'll be okay. You shouldn't care so much."

I didn't reply.

Cody gave me another curt nod and got into the driver's seat. He was always a man of few words.

I waved as I watched them drive down my gravel driveway until they were out-of-sight. I went back inside the Butterfly and shut the door. Asa was a grown woman. I had no control over her, but I felt she was in danger. Call it a mother's intuition.

30

Cody passed the Big House where only a few reporters remained camped on the side of the road. They seemed curious about the dark tinted SUV passing them. Some took phone snaps of the license plate.

"Airport, Boss?" Cody asked, careful to dodge the moving reporters.

Asa swallowed a pain pill she had in her pocket. "Yes, go toward the airport. I'm sure one of those reporters is going to follow us. Once we lose them, take me to the safe house."

"You're not leaving? I don't think that wise. You need rest."

"I'm going to finish what I started. I'm going to find Last Chance and root out the killer of Juan Gomez."

Cody clammed up. There was no use reasoning with Asa. He had worked for her many years. Once she got her teeth on a bone, she rarely let go.

Asa leaned back and rested her eyes. Cody was a

skilled operative, and she could relax in his care. The only thing Asa was not aware of was that her mother had put an air tag in her bag while she had been showering.

Sneaky, huh?

31

Yes, I put that air tag in my daughter's bag. Why? Because I don't trust Asa to tell me the truth. It wasn't that Asa was a liar. It was due to her job, whatever it was. I had a feeling her job's mantra was, *if I tell you, then I have to kill you.*

I checked the tracking app on my phone and to my surprise, the car was heading toward the airport. Regardless, I was going to keep an eye on my phone. Going toward the airport and getting on a plane are two different things.

It was time I got the move on. Bess had given me two addresses for Juan Gomez—one for his former residence with his wife and the other a rooming house on the north side of town. While Baby was sleeping, I sneaked out of the house and took off in my VW bus. I had already talked with Juan's wife. Now it was time to check out Juan's bachelor digs.

I developed a low-grade headache during the forty minutes to get across town. Ignoring the ever-so-slight pounding in my head, I parked on the street and stared blankly at the address. It was a ramshackle two-story, white frame house in serious need of repairs and a fresh coat of paint. To be honest it looked spooky—the kind of house where axe murders take place. I'm not kidding. I sat in the van wondering if I should go in. I didn't want to run into any drug addicts who would hit me over the head for the few dollars in my pocket. Taking a deep breath, I decided to go in—mainly because my van was creating attention. I saw people peeking out their windows. I would be quick in and quick out.

I walked with purpose toward the house with a clip board I kept in the van. It made me look like an official. At the very least, I could hit someone with it. It didn't take me very long to find Juan's room. It was the door with the yellow DO NOT ENTER tape crisscrossing it.

Reaching through the tape, I tried the door knob. The door was locked. Rats! I hate to be thwarted by such a minor inconvenience as a locked door. There was loud music playing down the hall. Hmm. Do I dare?

I knocked on the door where the music was playing. How bad could the occupant be? He or she was listening to George Jones, one of my favorite song birds. No one came to the door, so I knocked louder again.

Finally, I heard a shuffle of feet and heard someone say, "Who is it?"

"It's Mary Combs."

"Who?"

"Mary Combs. I need to get into Juan Gomez's apartment. Do you know of anyone who might have a key?"

The door opened slightly with the chain attached. The smell of bacon frying wafted through the open door as an elderly woman with cat-eye glasses peered out. George Jones wailed in the background. "I'm the supervisor of this apartment house. Why do you need to get into Mr. Gomez's apartment?"

I realized the lady must be from the mountains as she spoke with an Eastern Kentucky twang. I just lied right to this woman's face—again. "Hello. I'm Mary Combs. I am helping the family with the insurance policy. I need the key to get inside Mr. Gomez's room."

"If you're working with the insurance people, why don't you have the key?"

"We don't think the family would have the key as Mr. Gomez and his wife were estranged—and the police have not released Mr. Gomez's personal items such as his keys."

"Estranged, you say. I should say more like two enemies at battle with each other. Mrs. Gomez was always over here asking for money. Oh my goodness, the fights those two would have. One time I heard her say she wanted to kill him."

"She what?"

The woman asked, "Do you have any identification?"

Startled with the quick change of subject matter, I fumbled in my purse and got out my driver's license, flashing it quickly, not giving the woman enough time to read it. "You said Mrs. Gomez threatened to kill Mr. Gomez?"

"Wait a minute." The woman shut the door in my face. A few minutes later, she opened the door wearing a brightly-colored, floral caftan dress. She looked very festive. "I had to take dinner off the stove."

She pushed past me toward Juan Gomez's room.

"Do you own the building?"

"Lived here for over forty years."

Frustrated that the woman never seemed to answer my questions, I followed.

She pulled a key out of her pocket. "I don't know if I should let you in. The police still have their crime scene tape up."

"It's all right," I assured the lady. "This is just routine. I won't take long."

The caftan lady unlocked the door. "Here you go. Let me know when you leave. I'll need to lock it back up."

"Thank you, Mrs.—?"

"I'll be in my room if you need me—and leave the door open, dearie." Ignoring my question, she hurried back to her dinner of bacon and whatever.

Was her last name a secret? I was enamored by the caftan lady's technique of avoiding inquiries. She was brilliant at it. It's a skill I needed to hone.

Late afternoon shadows played on the walls of the hallway, and several people came in the back door, giving me a cursory glance before going to their rooms. It was getting late and people were getting home from work. Knowing I had to hurry, I ducked under the tape and entered the room. It was a sad little room with a stuffed chair by the window, a clock radio, and a chenille bedspread. The room looked like something out of the fifties. There was a small kitchenette by the door with a sink, two upper cabinets, three bottom cabinets, a college dorm refrigerator, and a hot plate. Near a small table sat a garbage can with takeout cartons spilled over onto the floor. The floor was covered by linoleum so old the linoleum skin had worn out in areas. A small bathroom was off to the side, while the main room served as the bedroom and living area. It was heartbreaking to see Juan Gomez reduced to living in this squalor. He must have missed his well-kept cheerful house with the colorful garden.

Since I was sure the police had been thorough, I skipped the usual places to look, concentrating on the back of pictures. Nope. Nothing taped there. Next I checked Juan's closet. I went through every coat and pants pocket. Even the toes of every shoe. It wasn't until I picked up Juan's fancy Tecovas cowboy boots and searched the toes that I found a sliver of paper. I had to gloat a bit, appreciating Detective Drake would have a spasm if he knew I found something his men did not.

Tee hee. Tee hee.

I unfolded the piece of paper to discover a series of numbers. I deduced that it was a phone number and must have been important for Juan to hide it like he did. I tucked it in my pocket before searching the rest of the room. I looked in the garbage, under the mattress, the kitchen table, and his stuffed chair. I'm pretty sure I hit all the spots the police had looked because I saw their fingerprint powder over everything. Good thing I wore gloves.

I looked out the window. It would soon be the gloaming of the evening. It was time to go.

I knocked on the caftan lady's door.

The caftan lady opened the door slightly. "Yes?"

"I'm finished, Mrs.—?" I had to try one more time.

"Okay."

Drat. She foiled me again.

I said, "You need to lock the door."

The woman stepped into the hallway. "I'll follow you out. Did you get everything you needed?"

As we both walked toward the front door of the

building, I asked, "Do you know why Mr. and Mrs. Gomez were separated?"

"It was because of Mrs. Gomez's gambling."

"You mean Mr. Gomez's gambling?"

Mrs. Caftan Lady stopped to lock Juan's door. She gave the doorknob a quick rattle to make sure. "No, it was due to his wife. She was a compulsive gambler. She liked to play the ponies."

I scribbled this down on my clipboard.

"Is that important?"

I looked up from my clipboard. "Yes. Very."

"Well, I could tell you stories."

Oh, please do. "Such as?"

The lady pushed her cat-eyed glasses back up her nose with her index finger. "Juan told me she stole his paychecks and gambled them all away. He had to leave so she wouldn't have access to his money. It got so bad with her gambling, Juan never had anything to eat at home because she lost the grocery money, the electricity was turned off, and finally, he skedaddled when some goon threatened to beat him up if Juan didn't cover his wife's bets."

"A bookie?"

"Yeah, one of those. Juan kept it a secret where he lived."

"But you said Mrs. Gomez visited Mr. Gomez here."

"That's right. She found out where he lived and was

causing trouble here. I told her if she came back I'd call the police on her. That stopped her visits, but that's the least of it."

"There's more?"

"One of Juan's sons visited about a month ago. Said he found a recent insurance policy taken out on his father by Mrs. Gomez. He wanted to know if Juan had signed off on that."

I leaned forward in anticipation.

Mrs. Caftan Lady said, "Juan hadn't. Knew nothing about an insurance policy making his wife the beneficiary. It really frightened him."

"What about the sons?"

"They are taking care of their mother. She is bleeding them dry like she did Juan, but what can you do? She's their mother."

"Have you seen them since their father died?"

"Nary a hair. But, of course, you must be investigating the insurance claim since you work for the insurance company."

"Yes. That's correct. Did you tell the police about the insurance policy?"

"They never asked."

I tried not to show my surprise. Drake was usually on the ball, but looked like he dropped it here. "Is there anyone else in the building who was close to Juan?"

"Just me. Juan worked nights. Most tenants work

during the day, so their paths didn't cross."

"You've been most helpful. Is there anything else you wish to tell me?"

The woman jabbed my chest with her finger. "You bet your bottom dollar that the hag of a wife had something to do with Juan's death."

I pushed her hand away as she was really poking me hard. "Just one more question. Did Juan ever talk about his car accident?"

Caftan Lady put her hands on her hips. "It was Mrs. Gomez who had the car accident. That's when her gambling started. She injured her brain. Juan said her personality changed after the accident."

Well, that lying . . . daughter-of-a-dog. I was completely fooled by Valeria Gomez, and she made me feel like a fool. I had been completely taken in by her performance.

I decided to take one last stab. "Just for my report, your name is?"

"Hazel Buford."

Success at last!

32

After thanking Hazel Buford, I headed toward my van. I had to get this information to Lady Elsmere and Shaneika Mary Todd, but first I checked the app on my phone. I needed to see if Asa had flown out of Lexington.

Guess what!

The little blinking dot showed me that Asa was encamped on Jacks Creek Pike, a road that runs perpendicular east of Tates Creek Road. The little stinker.

I called Bess and asked her to have her son run over to the Butterfly and let Baby out to tinkle. I didn't know when I would return home.

Bess assured me she would go over and bring Baby back with her. That was even better. She didn't inquire as to why I wouldn't be home, and I didn't confide in her.

I made a beeline to Jacks Creek Pike. I wasn't sure what I was going to find, but I had a deep suspicion I would find Asa—doing God knows what.

It was a little before dusk when I made my way to Jacks Creek Pike. As the road didn't have any lights, I had to find Asa before the sun went completely down. Otherwise I would have to go home and start again in the morning. With Asa, I wasn't sure she'd be in the same location come morning.

I was heading toward the river and dreaded driving down the steep incline which leads to the Kentucky River when the tag indicated the house on the right. I stopped the van and peered into the driveway, spying a little white framed house with a messy lawn. A car came up behind and honked his horn. I turned on my right blinker and turned cautiously toward the house. I stopped about fifty feet from the house and sat, gazing at the house.

A porch light came on.

Uh oh. What was I in for?

33

Asa stepped out on the porch while I climbed down from my van.

"How did you find me?" Asa asked, looking angry.

"What is this place, Asa?" I asked, glancing about.

Asa started to speak but then waved me inside. "If we're going to fight, let's do it in private."

I followed her inside, not knowing which one of us was the most hurt and incensed. The inside of the house was so different from the outside with nicely appointed rooms, freshly painted with refurbished wooden floors. I could see the kitchen through the living room arched doorway with its new appliances and gleaming white subway tiles. Cody sat at the kitchen table cleaning a gun.

"Cody, take a walk," Asa ordered.

He rose and walked out the kitchen door without saying a word.

"Sit down, Mother. Your leg is trembling. I'll get you something to drink."

"That would be nice," I muttered, rubbing my leg. I was feeling weak and pathetic.

Asa brought me bourbon with ice and a glass of water. "How did you find me?"

Ignoring her question, I tipped back the bourbon and wiped my mouth with the back of my hand. "You are always lying. I wanted to find out what you are up to."

Her voice very calm, Asa said, "Let's talk about lying. You want to tell me about your kidneys going bad."

"I'm fine," I shot back.

"No, you're not but we'll talk about that later."

"What is this place? What are you up to?"

"It's my safe house, but now I'll have to get another one since you've scoped this one out."

"But why? You can always stay with me."

"My work doesn't always permit me to stay with you. This hideaway is to protect you—and me."

"That sounds like you are in the Bluegrass more than you tell me."

Asa remained mute.

"Are you in the Bluegrass more than you tell me?"

"Mother, you've got to understand. My work does not make it permissible to share with you. It puts me in a precarious position. I've told you that before."

"But what is it that you do, Asa? Are you really an insurance investigator?"

"It is one of the jobs I have. That is true. I travel all over the world to investigate art fraud and to appraise art for insurance companies."

"What's the other part?"

"I have my own private consulting firm."

"To do what? Consult how?"

Asa put her hand on my arm. "I help. That's all I can tell you."

"Do you do illegal stuff? Immoral stuff?"

"Sometimes illegal, but never immoral I think. You instilled in me a bedrock ethical education as a child. I can still quote Bible verses, and I check in with God every now and then. I can tell you that I help people."

All I could think of was Denzel Washington. "Like the Equalizer?"

Asa tilted her head thinking. "Yes and no. I get paid for my interference unless the client is impoverished. Then I do pro bono, but I don't have many of those cases."

"How much is Lady Elsmere paying you?"

"Fifty thousand regardless of outcome and another fifty thousand if I find Last Chance in good condition."

I whistled. "You shook down the old woman."

"I didn't ask for anything. I would have done this case for free but she offered, so I took it. I'm not a saint and I have bills to pay."

"Isn't that the truth," I muttered under my breath. "I always thought you were more than an insurance agent. I thought you worked for the CIA."

"I do occasionally."

"And the military?" I remembered seeing a YouTube video of American nurses dancing in the Middle East with Asa handing a briefcase over to a military guy in the background. That video has since been scrubbed from the internet.

Asa nodded. "Now that's all I'm going to tell you. How did you track me down?"

"I put a tag in your bag," I announced proudly.

Asa went pale and blinked several times before she burst out laughing. "My own mother bested me, and you wonder where I get this urge to stick my nose in other people's business. Mom, you're the bomb!"

I didn't see what was so funny, but I joined in the laughter, too. I realized then I was relieved to see my daughter safe. I took a deep breath and then another until my low-grade headache disappeared. "I've got something to tell you."

"Yeah? Shoot!"

I told Asa of my visits with Renata, Valeria Gomez, and Hazel Buford. She listened carefully. It was dark when I finished.

Asa turned on some lights.

"So who is telling the truth?" I asked.

"That's hard to tell, but it puts a different spin on Juan's death."

"Detective Drake said something funny to me when

he was taking my statement. He asked me why I thought Juan's death was related to the kidnapping of Last Chance. I told him it was ridiculous to think they were not connected. Now I'm not so sure. Maybe they weren't."

"Let's look at this logically. Two women say that Juan had a gambling problem. One was Renata who stated she disliked the man because he criticized her. Maybe she heard bits of gossip and concluded it was Juan who was the gambler. Her dislike of the man colored her opinion."

"Renata wouldn't lie on purpose."

"I didn't say she did. I said she might have come to a wrong conclusion. You said she overhead the men talk in the shop but wasn't directly involved in the conversation."

I liked Renata and didn't want to see her name slighted. "I think that theory is farfetched but go ahead."

"Both Valeria Gomez's and Hazel Buford's stories contradict each other. Who has the most motive to lie?"

I said, "Let's say the insurance policy angle is true, then I would say Valeria Gomez."

"But Hazel Buford could have taken an illegal life insurance policy out on Juan without him knowing about it. Landlords do it all the time and then kill the victim."

"Insurance companies don't vet the policy holder? I don't think Hazel Buford is the guilty party here as she knew Juan had a family, who would come looking for him if missing."

Asa said, "Some companies require the holder's signature in person, but if an agent had never met Juan before, how would he know if the person signing was Juan Gomez or not?"

I asked, "Wouldn't the agent ask for identification?"

"Depends on how badly the agent wanted the commission."

"I was posing as an insurance investigator, and I flashed a phony badge. Mrs. Buford accepted it."

Asa interrupted me. "How ironic—you posing as me?"

"I used a different name, but I showed my driver's license with my real name and Hazel Buford accepted it. It's easy to flash something that looks like a badge. So you see it would be easy to lie to a lazy insurance agent who was eager to sell a policy." I paused for a moment.

Asa picked up an orange from a bowl on the coffee table and peeled it. She offered me a section which I turned down. "Tell me exactly what happened the morning you found Juan Gomez. Keep it concise."

"I joined Shaneika at the nursery barn. We went into the barn. Shaneika discovered Last Chance wasn't with his dam."

"Then what happened?"

"Shaneika searched the stalls."

"What did you do?"

"I had never seen the colt before, so I couldn't be of help."

"But you knew the colt had a white star and four white stocking feet. You stated in your police report you helped Shaneika recheck the stalls."

I didn't question how Asa got hold of the police report. "I guess I did now that I think of it."

"Was Jean Harlow's stall door closed?"

"Yes, she was in the stall and causing a raucous."

Asa asked, "Was Baby with you?"

"Yes."

"Did he show any signs of aggression toward anyone?"

"There was no one else in the barn."

"Then what?"

"Shaneika, Baby, and I went outside to look for the colt. Shaneika found Juan's car and ran up to the car, but Baby got there first. Shaneika pushed him away."

"So Baby got to the car first?"

"Yes, he raised his paws on the window ledge. Shaneika pushed him down."

"Okay, then what?"

"Shaneika was yelling at Juan, but he didn't answer. I opened the car door and he fell to the ground."

"Did you notice anything unusual—cigarette butts,

tools, tire tracks?"

I shook my head. "I knelt down and felt for a pulse. There was none and Juan felt cold. Shaneika called the police."

"Your story lines up with Shaneika's, but Drake must have found something to cause him to make that remark. I think he was fishing for more information."

I replied, "I was incensed that Drake thought the two crimes might not be connected. I'm afraid I was rather short with him. You think he may be right?"

"I'm wondering."

"Why don't you get your hacker to look in Juan's file? Aren't they all done by a computer now?"

"I'll check into it, but let's think about this. We assume Juan was killed by the kidnappers at the nursery barn. Yet he was getting ready to eat a candy bar and his gun was in his holster, so he was killed by someone he trusted or he didn't know the gunman was approaching."

"Wouldn't he see movement in his rearview or side mirrors? There are lights around the barn, so he wouldn't have been sitting in the dark."

"What if Juan was killed somewhere else on the farm and his car moved to the nursery barn. That would explain the scrubbing of the security tapes from the entire farm."

"There is nothing to support your theory, Asa."

"You think the police didn't find anything. You

don't know what they know."

"Asa, I can't seem to wrap my head around this one. It's too close to home."

"Did you find anything unusual in Juan's room?"

"I found this." I handed Asa the slip of paper with the numbers.

Asa studied the numbers and slumped back in her chair.

Alarmed, I asked, "Anything wrong? Don't you feel well?"

"I think you have discovered a possible connection to both the murderer and the kidnapping."

"Really?"

"Maybe, but it needs to be checked out. I want to speak with Lady Elsmere and formulate a plan."

"Why don't we just call the police?"

"Because we need the element of surprise." Asa rose and steadied herself by leaning against the back of the chair. "Mom, go home. I'll take care of this."

"Asa, I really think the police should be called."

"I'm going to, but first I have to talk with Shaneika and Lady Elsmere. We need to flush out the murderer or there is no use speaking to the police. We need proof. Mom, please go home and let me do my job."

I took a last sip of my drink and rose. "Call me?"

Asa gave a curt nod as I took my leave.

34

At ten forty-five the next morning, Lady Elsmere's lawyers agreed to turn over Jean Harlow, Comanche, and the stolen colt with his surrogate mare to Logan Kilkorn on the conditions that he never file a police report or pursue a civil suit and sign a non-disclosure agreement. Lady Elsmere authorized the legal document as did Shaneika.

The horses were to be delivered at Logan Kilkorn's farm at one-thirty that very day. Mike immediately got the vans ready for the horses while Shaneika cried on a few bales of hay in front of Comanche's stall.

I learned about the agreement when I went to pick up Baby. Charles was sitting at the kitchen table, looking gloomy, while Bess fluttered about the room like a distressed bird. The atmosphere in the room was thick. "What's happened?"

"Lady Elsmere and Miss Shaneika signed away Jean Harlow and Comanche," Bess uttered.

I looked in astonishment at Charles. "She didn't!"

"She had to if she wanted to save her reputation and the farm."

I said, "She could have fought it in court."

Charles snapped, "Again, we broke the law, Josiah. We stole Logan's colt. The man has us dead-to-rights. We would lose in both a criminal trial and civil suit. Her Ladyship is giving up her dream of a Kentucky Derby winner to save what's left of her legacy and the farm. She's trying to protect my family's future."

I placed my hand on Charles' shoulder. "I'm sorry. I know you had high hopes for that foal yourself."

Baby padded into the kitchen looking around for me. He must have heard my voice. His ears perked up as soon as he saw me and rushed over. I gave him a big hug. "I hope he wasn't too much trouble, Bess."

Bess deadpanned, "He just chewed up the end of an expensive Persian rug and tinkled in the hallway on the parquet floors."

My eyes must have widened to saucer size because Bess chuckled. "Gotcha!"

Relieved, I said, "You're a pill, Bess. I guess Lady Elsmere turning over the horses is a joke, too."

Charles rose from the table. "Nope. That's all too true." He went inside his office and shut the door.

Bess said, "It's really true, I'm afraid. It's not the end of the world, but my father doesn't agree."

I sank into a chair. I couldn't believe it. Shaneika was giving up Comanche—her dream horse and Lady

Elsmere was giving up Jean Harlow, whom she had paid millions for.

It was all too terrible to contemplate. "When are the horses going to be transferred?"

"This afternoon."

"This afternoon! Why so soon?"

"That's what the lawyers agreed upon."

I asked "Where is Lady Elsmere?"

"In the study with her lawyers."

"May I see her?"

"Let me check."

Bess picked up a house phone and pushed a button. A few seconds later she said, "Josiah is here." She listened for a heartbeat or two and then said, "I'll send her in." Putting down the receiver, Bess motioned toward the library. "Her Ladyship is waiting for you. Can you take this tray with you?"

"Sure." I picked up the tea tray with cheesecake brownie squares and black walnut cake slices. The library door was closed so I kicked the door with my foot. A middle-aged man answered and opened the door wide when he saw the tray. "Here, let me," he said, reaching for the tray.

"I've got it," I said, buzzing past him and setting the tray before Lady Elsmere.

"Josiah, I'd like you to meet my lawyers. These gentlemen handled all my unpleasant legal issues." She gave me their names, but I don't remember them.

"This is my next door neighbor, Josiah Reynolds."

They apparently knew who I was as their eyes looked me up and down but not in a flattering way.

Lady Elsmere said, "Boys, stop by the kitchen and take a piece of cake with you. I'll see you both at Logan Kilkorn's."

Seeing that they had been dismissed, the lawyers lumbered out of the room, shutting the door behind them. Lady Elsmere ordered, "Josiah, pour two cups of tea please, and I want both the cheesecake and the black walnut cake."

I did as bidden and handed her a plate with several slices of cake and two cheesecake brownies. "Well, it seems like losing Jean Harlow has not dampened your appetite."

"I'm not going to lose Jean Harlow."

"How's that?"

"Asa called last night. She says she should have figured it out before, but she wasn't thinking clearly due to her injury."

"Figured what out?"

"Come with me to Logan J. Kilkorn's farm and see for yourself. And bring Baby, too."

"You want me to bring a Mastiff to a strange horse farm?"

"Baby likes horses, doesn't he?"

"Yes, but will Kilkorn's horses like him? It's dangerous bringing a strange dog around horses."

Lady Elsmere took a bite of her cake and just gave me a little Mona Lisa smile. I knew she had something up her sleeve, but what did it have to do with my dog?

I guess I'd have to wait until the afternoon.

35

It was raining hard when we left for Logan J. Kilkorn's farm. I saw employees gathering our horses to take them back to the barns. Horses were moved inside when lightning was a threat.

I sat in the back of the Bentley with Baby, Lady Elsmere, and Shaneika as Charles drove the car. Behind the Bentley were two horse trailers—one carrying Logan Kilkorn's foal with its surrogate dam and another carrying Jean Harlow with a companion goat. Lady Elsmere's lawyers rode in a silver Lexus behind the trailers. After a half hour, our little caravan pulled up to the Kilkorn estate.

Charles blew the horn and a gatekeeper rushed out to open the large metal gates guarding the farm. He stopped once inside the gate and asked for the nursery barn. The gatekeeper gave him directions, saying the Kilkorns were waiting for the horses.

It was still thundering and yellow lightning streaked through the gray sky. The world looked ominous.

"You know it's not too late to turn around and fight to keep these horses," I said, losing my nerve. "It's madness to give Kilkorn Jean Harlow."

Lady Elsmere held up her hand. "Steady on, Josiah. All will be revealed."

I held my tongue but it was hard. I thought this a dreadful mistake.

We finally made it to the nursery barn where Logan and Micah Kilkorn waited for us inside. The horse trailers, including our cars, pulled directly into the dry barn to escape the downpour.

The drivers exited their vehicles. Lady Elsmere, Shaneika, the lawyers, and I, with Baby on a leash, did the same.

Logan Kilkorn held up his hand. "What do you think this is—a parade?"

Lady Elsmere answered, "Ms. Todd and I would like to make sure the transfer goes smoothly. We don't want to have you accuse us of the horses not being in one hundred percent condition when delivered."

"That makes sense, but what's the dog doing here? I don't like dogs around my horses. It makes them jumpy."

Shaneika spoke, "This dog is a companion for Jean Harlow. He calms her."

"You mean the dog stays with her?" Micah Kilkorn asked.

"No, but the dog will help her get settled," Lady

Elsmere said. "Let me introduce you to the owner of the dog—Josiah Reynolds, my next door neighbor."

"I know who she is. Seen her picture in the paper. She's always stumbling over dead bodies. Can we get on with this?" Logan asked impatiently and apparently dismissing me.

"And these are my lawyers giving you a copy of our agreement," Lady Elsmere said, graciously."

Logan snatched the two copies presented and checked for signatures. Seeing that Shaneika and Lady Elsmere had signed and dated the contract, Logan looked at the trailers with interest. "Where's the stallion, Comanche?"

"He has a cover this afternoon. He'll be free tomorrow," Shaneika replied.

"I want him first thing in the morning. I'm already scheduling covers."

Shaneika suggested, "Let's get the colt settled."

A groom stepped up to help, but Lady Elsmere rebuffed him. "We'll do this, son."

The groom glanced at Logan Kilkorn who gave a nod to step back.

Charles and the driver of the horse van opened the back of the trailer. The driver led a mare from the vehicle into the barn aisle. Then Asa stepped down from the van leading the rambunctious colt.

"Who the hell is she?" Logan asked Micah.

Micah recognized Asa and blurted out. "That's Billy.

A girl I met at a bar a few days ago." He glanced sideways at his father. He didn't want his dad to know that was the night the colt was stolen.

Logan looked confused. "What's she got to do with our colt, son?"

Asa brought the colt before the two men. "I'm the one who stole him, sir."

Logan grew angry. "I'll have you arrested then."

Asa wagged a finger. "No, you won't. You signed an agreement—no police if your colt was returned by one-thirty today."

Logan and Micah gave quick glances at their watches.

"You have the contracts given to you by one-fifteen, signed, sealed, and delivered. However, we can have you both arrested," Asa reminded Logan.

Logan yelled at Lady Elsmere, who was now sitting in a wheelchair in front of the Bentley. "June, what BS is this? We had a deal." He tossed both contracts away from him.

Charles wheeled Lady Elsmere closer to Logan and Micah.

She said, "Logan, listen to me. It will be to your benefit. I don't think you realize that you are being hoodwinked. If I leave here and press charges, you will be banned from every racetrack for life."

"Ridiculous."

Lady Elsmere said, "Just listen. Asa, tell Logan

what's going on."

"Get on with it then," Logan said, grudgingly. He didn't like Lady Elsmere, but he respected her.

The foal was skittish, so Asa turned him over to Charles who held fast to his halter. "The plan was so simple, that I completely dismissed it out-of-hand. It was brilliant, Micah."

Micah glanced nervously at his father. "I don't know what you are talking about."

"It's about switching colts. This little guy is a good horse, but he's not a great horse like Last Chance."

Logan took a hard look at the colt. "This horse is not ours. We don't have a colt with these markings."

"But the white star and the stocking feet are the markings of Last Chance," Asa replied.

"I don't know what's going on here," Logan said, looking flummoxed. "Why did you bring me this colt, June?"

Lady Elsmere answered, "Because he is your colt, Logan—disguised as Last Chance."

Asa said, "Let me prove it to you. According to the agreement, we are returning your colt."

Shaneika stepped forward and sprayed a solution on a towel while reassuring the Kilkorns. "This won't hurt the foal at all. It's liquid detergent with baking soda." She rubbed the towel over the horse's forehead. "I think you can see for yourselves now."

Logan Kilkorn peered closer. "His star is coming

off. He's been dyed!"

"Exactly. To match Last Chance's marking. Now take your chip wand."

The groom handed Logan the chip wand which he waved over the horse. A beep went off.

Lady Elsmere said, "I would like my lawyers to verify that the chip contains information that states this horse belongs to the Logan J. Kilkorn. Gentlemen, verify." She waved them toward Logan and the wand.

"May we, sir?" they asked politely, taking the wand from Logan. They took a picture of the information on their phones and returned the wand to Logan.

Asa said, "Mr. Kilkorn, you look puzzled. Let me clarify the events of the past few days. How often do you come to the nursery barn?"

"I don't. The colts and fillies are my son's responsibilities. I handle the training of the juveniles and up."

"Do you know how many foals were birthed this spring?"

"Seven of our own."

"And those seven would be in this barn?" Asa asked.

"We keep our stock away from other owners' horses."

"Like Lady Elsmere, you board horses for other people?"

"Yes, but we keep only our foals in this barn."

Asa said, "Very good. Then you should have only

six foals with their dams right now—this little guy being your foal. Would you count the number of foals you have in the stalls right now?"

"Of all the foolishness," Logan muttered, abruptly turning and strutting about the barn counting the foals inside the stalls. He came back looking sheepish and rubbing his chin in dismay.

"What did you find, Logan?" Lady Elsmere asked.

"Seven foals."

Asa remarked, "But if I stole your colt, which I admit that I did, then you should have only six foals. Right?"

Logan shot his son a hard look. "That would seem so."

Asa continued, "I propose that a switch took place between your foal and Last Chance. Shall we continue with the experiment?"

Logan agreed. "By all means. Let's get to the bottom of this."

When Micah began slowly drifting away from the group, Logan grabbed his arm. "Where are you going, son? Don't you want to see what these folks have up their sleeves?"

"I have paperwork to do, Dad. You can handle this."

"It can wait, boy. You stand right next to me," Logan ordered before turning to Asa. "Proceed, young lady. You seem to be in charge here."

Asa nodded to Charles who let go of the colt.

Everyone held their breath watching as to what the colt would do next.

36

The colt went over to his surrogate mother and began nursing.

Lady Elsmere suggested, "Logan, have your groom take the colt and his surrogate mother to a stall away from the other horses. We don't want these horses further confused."

The groom walked the unruffled dam to a stall with the colt duly following. As soon as they were out-of-sight, Asa told Shaneika to bring out Jean Harlow.

Shaneika opened the trailer doors and, with the driver's help, led Jean Harlow out along with her companion goat. The scents of unfamiliar mares and the sight of a strange barn unnerved Jean Harlow, making her hard to manage. The driver and Charles had to help Shaneika calm the mare while the goat looked about for something to munch on, but that is the nature of a goat.

Lady Elsmere asked, "Logan, do you acknowledge this horse as Jean Harlow?"

Logan answered, "I was at Keeneland when you overpaid for her. Yes, this is Jean Harlow."

"To confirm the horse's identity, please read her tattoo number aloud and wand her for the chip. My lawyers have her racing papers verifying the tattoo number."

Logan said, "June, I've already concurred this horse is Jean Harlow."

"I want it officially on record that you have read the tattoo number and wanded her."

Begrudgingly, Logan went over to Jean Harlow and lifted her quivering lip. "Whoa, girl. Just taking a quick peep." He read the numbers which the lawyers confirmed were correct. Then he waved the wand over the horse. The digital data verified the horse was Jean Harlow and the legitimate owner was Lady Elsmere.

"Now what?" Logan asked.

"Now the dog comes into it," Asa said. "Mrs. Reynolds, let Baby loose, please."

Baby's ears perked up at the mention of his name. He no doubt thought a treat would be in the offing. I dropped the leash.

Happy to be unfettered, Baby shuffled up to Asa, who gave him a dry biscuit. Curious about the unfamiliar barn, the English Mastiff looked about, sniffing the air.

"That's right, Baby. Smell something familiar? Go find Last Chance," Asa said, giving his collar a tug.

Baby slowly walked with Asa past the stalls until he stopped at one and barked, eagerly wagging his tail.

A small whinny sounded above the closed stall door.

Asa asked, "Please open this stall door and keep the dam inside. We want to see what the foal will do."

Logan ordered Micah to open the stall door.

"Dad, can I talk to you alone?" Micah, pleaded with his father.

"Not now. We are going to see this through. Do what I tell you."

Micah approached the stall as though walking to his doom. He opened the stall door and quickly leashed the dam's halter to a hook so she wouldn't follow the colt.

Baby immediately rushed into the stall, pushing Micah aside.

Logan cried out, running toward the stall, "STOP HIM!"

Asa held out her hand. "It's okay, Mr. Kilkorn. It's okay. See."

An ebony colt emerged from the stall kicking and bucking while Baby followed giving a playful chase. The colt stopped momentarily to nibble from a pail of sweet feed left out, giving Baby the opportunity to lick him. The colt darted away, looking back to see if Baby was following him. Baby was about to give chase when Asa brought him to a halt.

"Baby, sit," Asa ordered, giving him a treat. "Good boy."

At the sight of the colt darting about, Jean Harlow sniffed the air and grew more agitated. She neighed and kicked while Charles and the driver struggled to contain her.

The colt raised his head and whinnied back, looking curiously at the horse held by two men. He cautiously ambled toward Jean Harlow, who was trying to pull away from her restraints.

Shaneika quickly grabbed the colt's halter and rubbed her damp towel on the colt's forehead and held it out for all to see—the towel was saturated with black dye. A partial white star stood out on the colt's forehead.

Last Chance had been found!

37

All hell broke loose, let me tell you.

Asa unhooked the surrogate dam and slammed her stall door shut. I ran over and grabbed Baby and pushed him into a stall, afraid he was going to be trampled on during the confusion. Shaneika got kicked by Last Chance, who was frightened by Jean Harlow's fierceness, although she managed to grab the colt's halter and shove him into the stall with Baby. Charles and both drivers did the same with Jean Harlow. They put her in a stall next to Last Chance where mother and son could see each other.

The barn erupted in a cacophony of neighs and whinnies as all the mares were now upset which caused their babies to be disturbed as well.

Logan summoned his farm manager on his phone. He needed help in the nursery barn ASAP.

Lady Elsmere wheeled over to Logan. "It's time you and I have a come-to-Jesus-meeting. You need to hear the entire story."

Logan nodded and yelled for Micah, looking about the barn.

Feeling lightheaded, Asa gently sat on a hay bale and informed Logan, "I'm afraid Micah's not here, Mr. Kilkorn. He took off during the melee. I think I hear his Alpha Romeo Spider zooming away now, but don't worry. My men will catch Micah and bring him back. Of course, his car might be a little banged up, but that's to be expected."

Lady Elsmere said, "Logan, let's all go to your house and have a drink. I'm parched after all this excitement. What do you say?"

Logan seemed worried but replied, "By all means. I need someone to tell me what's going on?"

In a lucky break, the rain let up although the sky was still cloudy. At least the lightning had stopped threatening us. Charles wheeled Lady Elsmere alongside Logan while Asa tagged along.

Shaneika put Jean Harlow's companion goat in with her. We both filled the horses' water buckets and put sweet feed in the stalls. We were about to make our way up to the house, when stable hands arrived to move Logan's horses into the pastures since the storm had moved on.

Once those horses were removed, our horses would calm down.

I made sure the grooms understood they were not to release Jean Harlow and her colt. Of course, seeing

Baby in the stall with the colt would deter anyone from letting the colt loose.

Shaneika decided to stay in the barn and guard the horses. I told her to call if she needed anything. I didn't think we'd be long for I was sure Kilkorn would want us to leave after Asa related her story.

But I was thirsty and needed something to wash down all this horse dandruff tickling my throat. I went to the Kilkorn's antebellum mansion and let myself in.

Everyone was in the study drinking highballs and bourbon mules except for Asa, whom I saw sneak a pain pill from her pocket and wash it down with warm water. I understood the awful power of pain, so I said nothing. I had been a pain pill junkie myself for years.

She sat in a chair commanding the entire group: Logan, Charles, Lady Elsmere, the two lawyers, and now myself. "Mr. Kilkorn, would you rather I speak to you alone? What I'm about to tell you is rather heartbreaking."

"Let's have at it," Logan said. He ran his hand across his mouth.

"All right," Asa said. "I stole your foal because I thought it was Last Chance. I found the horse in your root cellar by your abandoned frame house."

Logan slapped his knee. "That's preposterous. No one puts a foal in a root cellar."

"I have proof, sir." Asa showed Logan footage on her phone of going into the cellar and finding the colt.

The man seemed astonished. "Who would do such a thing and why?"

"For the same reason someone would dope a competitor's horse when he knew the horse would be tested before the race and traced back to your stables. It was to incriminate someone," Asa replied.

Logan hung his head.

Lady Elsmere wheeled over to him. "You didn't order the doping of your competitor's horse, did you?"

When Logan didn't respond, Asa answered for him. "We all know it was Micah, and you took the blame for the incident blemishing your reputation for all time."

"He's my son. My only son."

"And your love for your son cost you a two year ban from racing. That's what started this entire mess. At first, I thought it was due to you opposing Lady Elsmere's activism, but then I realized it had to do with greed."

Logan looked up—first at Lady Elsmere, who nodded affirmatively, and then at Asa who studied him quietly with those dark eyes of hers.

Asa said, "You may not want to admit this about your only son, but Micah is dangerous, and I think you've known it for a long time."

"What are you trying to tell me, lady?"

"Micah used the excuse of your feud with Lady Elsmere to cover up his plot to steal Last Chance. Why would he do that? Because he was furious the doping scheme only caused you minimal penalties, and he needed a way to get your foot off his neck. He wanted to take over the Kilkorn estate and get you out of the way."

"But I'm his father. He would betray his own father over a bunch of horses!"

Asa replied, "Yes, he would, Mr. Kilkorn. I've shown you the video of me finding your colt in the root cellar. You know that's your root cellar. You can go right now to that cellar and find straw and manure on the floor."

Kilkorn murmured, "I believe you."

Lady Elsmere interjected, "We believe Micah hoped this entire incident would blow up in both our faces. He was hoping you would make this a criminal matter and when it came out that you had stolen Last Chance, you would be banned from racing for life. If for some reason, Last Chance had an accident or died, competition for the Kentucky Derby in two years would be lessened. Again, Micah came out ahead. If Last Chance lived and nothing was discovered, then he would run Last Chance as his horse in the Derby. Again, he would be in control of the Kilkorn estate, his father banned from racing, and he would be king of the hill."

"What's going to happen here on out?" Logan asked.

Charles answered, "Like you, we want to keep this incident quiet. The scandal would be bad for business.

We have written up an agreement that states we won't press charges if you return Last Chance, and you will have no more claims over Jean Harlow and Comanche. Micah will sign an affidavit stating your involvement in the kidnapping of Last Chance. You will absolve Lady Elsmere, the Dupuy family, and Shaneika Mary Todd of any criminal prosecution regarding this and future legal actions, including civil suits. In other words, we will be beyond your legal reach."

"What else?" Logan sneered.

"You are to quit harassing me at public venues and in private. I know what you say about me," Lady Elsmere said.

Logan said, "If you get your reforms, owners of small horse farms will have to sell out because they won't be able to compete. The days of a lone breeder making his way to the Triple Crown will be over. The farms will be gobbled up by developers who will pave the Bluegrass into one big shopping mall. You want to see that happen?"

"No, I don't, Logan, but I want to see this cruelty in racing brought to an end. It must be stopped if we are to save the sport," Lady Elsmere confessed.

"It's not the horses that are important, June. It is the land. The Bluegrass is a special ecosystem. The horses are key to keeping this region intact. Once the horses are gone, the land will be gone, too. Don't you see that? It's the land that's important. It must be preserved."

"Then work with me to achieve your goal. Between the two of us, we can accomplish both our dreams," Lady Elsmere said.

"Work with you? That would cause a lot of raised eyebrows."

"What have you got to lose, Logan?" Lady Elsmere asked.

"My son, June. What's gonna happen to my son?"

Asa intervened, "I'm afraid we can't help where the death of Juan Gomez is involved. If he's guilty of killing Gomez, he will have to pay the price, but you must accept that Micah is involved. Maybe he set this scheme up?"

Logan scoffed, "Micah set this kidnapping up? He doesn't have the brains for it. Listen, my son is a weak man, but he's not a killer."

"Your son was willing to let you take the blame for his horse doping and then freeze you out of your own property," Asa replied. "Let that sink in."

"Did my son kill your man, June?"

Lady Elsmere turned to Asa. "Did Micah?"

"I know he was involved, but I don't think he actually pulled the trigger."

Logan sighed with relief and pointed at Asa. "I don't know who you are, but if you can prove someone else is responsible for Gomez's murder, I'll pay you twenty thousand dollars."

"Lordy, you're cheap," Lady Elsmere muttered.

"I'm paying her one hundred thousand."

"Agreed," Asa said, holding out her hand, ignoring Lady Elsmere.

Logan shook it. "Are we done here?" he asked.

One of the lawyers handed Logan a contract. "Sign this and we're done."

"I'll have my lawyer look at it."

"No, Logan," Lady Elsmere said, "Sign now or the deal is off. We need to make an end to this calamity. My nerves can't take any more."

A lawyer handed Logan J. Kilkorn a pen. "Sign here, sir, at the yellow arrow and then put the date with the time."

Logan took a deep breath and signed the contract. "I'm trusting you to keep your word, June."

"These boys will mail you copies of the new agreement," Lady Elsmere said. "We'll be on our way after we collect our animals. Oh, Logan, I'm leaving the surrogate dam here for your colt in case his real mother rejects him, but that dam is still mine. As soon as your colt weans, I'll be back for her."

"Noted," replied Logan. "Now if you don't mind, I won't see you out. Don't let the door hit you in the fanny, June."

Taking that as a firm *get out of my house* request, I rose from my chair and was the first one out of the door. Charles took Lady Elsmere straight home, while Asa and I stayed behind to help Shaneika and the drivers collect the horses.

Last Chance was put in a van with Baby and Shaneika, keeping it company while Asa sat in front with the driver. It drove off first as I and the other driver wrestled with Jean Harlow. Oh, how I wanted to punch that stupid mare for she was being so difficult, but what good would that do? After twenty minutes of hassling with her, we resorted to using the goat and sweet feed as bait to get Jean Harlow into the remaining van. I could see why Lady Elsmere said this was the last time she was going to breed her. Jean Harlow was too high maintenance.

We finally got her into the van, and the driver slammed the door shut. We shook hands at our success. Happily, we drove to Lady Elsmere's farm without incident. When we got there, Mike met us at the gate and instructed the driver to go to a special barn. He jumped on the running board as we drove to the barn.

There Last Chance was already ensconced in a special stall with a metal half wall between him and the other stall. An adult horse could lean her head over the wall but not low enough to hurt a foal.

Shaneika was giving the colt some mash mixed with my honey. She looked up and smiled when she heard us coming in. I could tell she was at peace, having found the colt. I was happy for her.

Mike led Jean Harlow into the opposite stall. Immediately, she began pacing the floor.

I watched the mare's agitated movements. "What now, Mike?"

"Let's hope the smell of her foal increases her hormone levels, and she'll accept Last Chance. Meanwhile, we'll bottle feed him. I need to prepare a bottle. Excuse me."

"I'm taking off. Where's Asa and Baby?"

Shaneika answered, "We left them at the Butterfly."

I said, "I'm taking the golf cart outside the barn, Shaneika."

"Okay, I'll tell someone at the Big House you took it."

"Thanks." I paused. "Shaneika?"

"Yeah?" She looked up at me as Last Chance snatched the bucket away from her.

"I'm glad you found Last Chance. I really am."

Shaneika gave me a big sloppy grin as she bent over to retrieve the bucket.

I left the barn feeling better than I had in a week. I was glad the kidnapping and the murder were behind us. The police can handle the murder as it was out of our hands now.

First thing I did was to check on that hive with the swarm. It was doing great. The bees looked healthy bringing in lots of pollen on their back legs. A good number of guards met the field bees flying in. That meant the hive was in good shape. I would give it a couple of more days before I opened it to see if the queen was laying. Good so far.

I parked the cart in front of the Butterfly, and as soon as I opened the front door, Baby met me at the door, wagging his tail. A cacophony of cats meowed and trailed behind. Oh, dear, Asa had let the Kitty Kaboodle in. I hoped they hadn't knocked anything over or deposited something nasty on my slate floors.

"Asa," I called out.

Silence.

"Asa?" I cried, searching the rooms.

Asa was nowhere to be seen.

She was gone.

38

I was so angry I could hardly breathe. I had put up with this type of behavior from Asa's father. I was not going to put up with this passive-aggressive crap from my daughter.

Immediately, I jumped into my van and drove over to her "safe house." I was floored to see a FOR SALE sign in the yard. I got out of my van and tried the door. It was locked with one of those realtor key safes on the knob. Peeking in the windows, I could see the house had been stripped bare—no furniture and no drapes. I checked the mail box. Nothing.

Asa was gone.

I sat on the porch steps in bewilderment.

Like Jesus, I wept.

39

Dandy Dan got in his black 1967 Ford Cortina a happy man. He had just made a killing on a bet and was thinking of flying to London to have several suits made by his tailor on Savile Row. He eased into the front seat and pulled his keys from his pocket.

"Leave it."

Startled, Dan glanced in his rearview mirror to see Asa sitting in his back seat. She was wearing all black leather and sporting large sunglasses. She even had on leather gloves. Not a good sign.

Seeing Dan flinch, looking wildly around the Keeneland parking lot, Asa said, "Don't try to flee, Dan. My men will block you. See them?"

Dan glanced out his car window to see several men also dressed in black hulking about his car.

"Besides we punched your tires. All four are flat or they will be shortly."

"You didn't?" He hated that he couldn't see Asa's eyes. He was good at spotting when people were lying.

"I did, Dan." She got out of the back and plastered herself in the passenger's seat.

"You know what they call women like you?" Dan said, heatedly.

"Yeah. Resourceful."

"What do you want this time?"

"A confession."

Dan snorted. "To what?"

"The kidnapping of Last Chance and the murder of Juan Gomez."

"In your dreams, Asa. You can't prove a thing."

"I see you're not denying it."

"Like I said, you can't prove a thing."

"But I can, Dan. You see the police found a sliver of paper with your phone number on it in the toe of Mr. Gomez's Tecovas boots. The phone number connects you to him. The popo are going to be coming your way soon," Asa bluffed as she hadn't turned the paper over to the police yet. She had to make sure Dan was guilty first.

Dan said hastily, "Let me explain. It wasn't my fault." He changed his tone of voice to one of silky smoothness. "You know I can be quite an asset to your organization. Oh, I know all about you."

Asa's heart sank for now she knew Dan was involved. "If you know all about me, you would know that I have security clearance at the highest levels. You can't touch me. You can't hurt me, but I can hurt you,

Dan. All I have to do is put out on the streets that you snitched. If I were you, I would take my chances with the police."

Dan licked his lips. "Let's not be impetuous, Asa. Other than a piece of paper with my number, I don't have any connection to Gomez's murder. Sure he had my number. I was his wife's bookie and sometimes, he came through and paid her marker. That's all there was between us."

"Here's how I think it went down, Dan." Asa scooted over and put her arm around Dan's shoulder, pulling him close. "Valeria Gomez used you as her bookie. You let her get deeper and deeper into debt until she was beyond redemption. She mentioned her husband, Juan, worked for Lady Elsmere and her prize mare had just given birth to a foal with remarkable markings and a broad chest. Everyone thought this foal was going to be a Kentucky Derby contender. In fact, Lady Elsmere was counting on it."

"Lots of horses are Kentucky Derby contenders. Means nothing."

Asa continued, "Then there is Micah Kilkorn. I bet he couldn't keep his mouth shut about resenting his father, complaining all over town. He wanted the old man out of the way. You heard about his rage, so you approached him with a plan. If your plan succeeded, you would have a percentage on the Kilkorn winner's purses and stud fees. With Logan out of the way, Micah would be free to race the horses again, and you thought owning a stake in a horse is more satisfying than betting on one. You'd get to lounge in a sky box at the Derby instead of jostling with the great unwashed at the pari-mutuel windows."

"Oh, Asa, how you do go on. Prattle. Nothing but prattle. You should really see a shrink. You're positively paranoid."

"Once you made a deal with Micah, you had to figure out a plan to get rid of his old man. You already had Valeria Gomez in your pocket and squeezing her husband for every dime you could get out of him. I guess you finally approached Juan with the idea that if he gave you the codes to Lady Elsmere's security gates you would wipe out his wife's markers and not take any more bets from her."

Dan insisted, "You're wasting both of our time. Get out of my car before you make more of a fool out of yourself."

Asa squeezed Dan's shoulder until he gave a little squeal. "You like pretty things, and you need money for that. This was your chance of moving up a notch. Having Juan Gomez at your mercy was too much of a temptation. You could become a real player, but you were too greedy, my friend. Too greedy."

Dan pushed Asa's hand away from him. "I know you're recording our conversation. I'm not going to admit to anything because you're wrong. I had nothing to do with Juan Gomez's death."

Asa whispered into Dan's ear. "Once Valeria realizes that you're not going to take her bets any longer, she will turn on you and report you to the police. Her sons are a different matter though. They look like good strong men who know how to throw a punch or two. It will be interesting to see how this will play out—will Valeria report you as suspicious in her husband's death or will the sons beat you to a pulp?"

Dan withdrew a handkerchief from his vest pocket and wiped his hands.

"Then there is Micah Kilkorn. He's already thrown in the towel and fled. It appears Logan Kilkorn knew nothing about the horse swap. When I showed him a video of finding his foal in the root cellar on his property, he was pretty pissed. However, Logan still loves his son. He's paying me twenty thousand dollars to prove that Micah didn't kill Juan Gomez. I plan to collect the twenty thousand dollars, even though Micah might still go down as an accessory to murder. That leaves you hanging for Murder One. You're the one who pulled the trigger. Why, Dan? Juan was an old man."

"Stop it, Asa." Sweat beaded on Dan's brow.

"You went alone that night. First thing you needed to do was dismantle the security system. Didn't you tell me that you kept your hand in where computers are concerned? Juan had a key to the Big House in case of an emergency which you used to gain entrance to the computers. You wiped all the security footage clean—even the cloud. Then you gave Juan his key and watched him put the key back before you shot him. My guess is that the two you got into an argument—perhaps Juan wanted the money back he paid you over the last several years or maybe he had lost his nerve and wanted to nix the deal. In any event, you shot him and then put his body into his car. That's why there was very little blood in his car."

Dan protested, "Here's a hole in your theory. I don't own a horse trailer and I certainly didn't borrow one, so how did I whisk Last Chance away?"

"He's a little guy. All you had to do was pick him up and put him in a SUV or something similar. He would have lain down. You took him to Micah and the rest is history."

"Quite an imagination, Asa. You should write mystery novels."

"You keep saying that, but you're not saying I am wrong. You're as guilty as hell."

Dan suddenly grabbed at Asa, scratching her face. She thrust her elbow upwards into his solar plexus filling the car with a loud whoosh as Dan had the wind knocked out of him.

Asa's operatives responded a few seconds later, ripping the car door open and pulling Dan out of the Cortina, ready to pulverize him.

"Don't, boys. Let's not cause a scene. People are milling about." She and her men walked over to a black SUV parked nearby and got in. Asa blew Dan a kiss as they passed him writhing on the ground.

As her vehicle passed by, Dan thought he was going to kill Asa one day if he survived this. It was a solemn promise he made to himself!

40

Life goes on. It was several days later when I was browsing through my DVD collection in search of a 40s noir film to watch with Matt when a blaring car horn shattered the peace of my farm. Who was that disturbing my animals?

I opened the front door in a huff and saw Asa standing by a black Jeep with a huge smile on her face. I was filled with a mixture of delight and boiling anger. How could Asa drop off the face of the earth one day and then pop up unannounced the next?

I said, "I thought you had absconded for parts unknown."

"I thought about it, but I knew it would make you angry."

"How sharper than a serpent's tooth it is to have a thankless child."

Asa replied, "Act I, Scene 4 of King Lear."

"You got that right, daughter of mine. Hey, what happened to your face?"

"A cat scratched me."

"Okay, if that's the way you want to play it."

"That's how I want to play it." Asa laughed. "You're nosy, you know."

I didn't return the laughter as I was not amused. "Now what?"

"I think it is time I take a vacation."

"Really?" I replied, folding my arms.

"There a dinky little motel in Key Largo. Actually it's a very nice motel—mid-century with all the modern conveniences. I think you would like it—for a week or so. They even have manatees." She looked at me expectantly. "You want to go—with me?"

It took me a few seconds to respond as Asa caught me by surprise. "I'll take a week—or so with you. You know I love manatees. You are inviting me to take a vacation with you?"

"Yep."

"Maybe I'd like to go."

"Good. It's settled. We're leaving now."

"Now?"

"Yes."

"Like right now?"

"Grab a toothbrush and some undies and let's go."

"I can't, Asa. I have to make arrangements for the animals. Can't do it on a moment's notice."

"I've already arranged with Charles to take care of the stable and the rest of your menagerie."

"There's Baby to consider." I felt crushed. I really wanted to go.

"Bring Baby along."

"The plane won't accept a two hundred pound dog in the main cabin, and I won't put him in cargo storage."

"I've got a hundred and twenty thousand dollars burning a hole in my pocket. I have chartered a private plane. There's chilled champagne and a charcuterie board waiting for us. Baby will be flying first class." Asa clapped her hands. "Now, let's go, woman. Time's a wastin'."

I ran inside and grabbed my toothbrush, clean underwear, and my phone, tossing them in my purse. I roused Baby from his nap and snapped a leash on his collar. He lumbered after me looking very puzzled. Oh, yeah, I snatched a box of treats for him which I could not stuff in my purse.

I put Baby in the back of the Jeep and jumped in the passenger's seat, slamming the door. I was so excited to be going to the Keys with my daughter. The last time we were there, I had been recuperating from my fall.

Asa turned on the Jeep and drove down the gravel driveway.

"So you proved Micah did not kill Juan Gomez—hence the extra twenty thousand?"

"He was involved in the scheme to kidnap Last

Chance, but he wasn't even there when the kidnapping went down. I reported him and his whereabouts to the police—an anonymous tip. When the police catch up with him, he'll spill his guts—he's such a flibbetygibbet."

"And Logan will hire a white shoe lawyer and get him off."

"Probably."

"Who did kill Juan Gomez if not Micah?"

"I'll tell you on the plane over drinks. It's a long involved story. It should last us our plane trip." Asa punched in the code to open the gate to Tates Creek Road. "We really have to get going. We don't want the champagne to get warm."

"I see you have the safe house up for sale."

"You blew my cover. Had to."

"Sorry about that."

Asa chuckled. "Look at your lying face in the mirror. No, you're not."

"No, I'm really not," I confessed. "I think it was awful of you to flit in and out of the Bluegrass and not come to see me."

"I'm not gonna argue about this. It was for your own protection."

We sat in silence until Asa asked, "What about Last Chance? Did Jean Harlow ever accept him again?"

"Begrudgingly at first, but I think they are a tight bond now. However, Shaneika is keeping a close eye on them."

Asa asked, "Are they going to wean Last Chance in a couple of months?"

"Lady Elsmere and Shaneika are going to try a different method of raising him. They are going to keep those two together for a much longer time. They want to see if that will lessen the trauma for Last Chance when he starts his training."

"What do you think his prospects of becoming a Kentucky Derby contender?"

"The same as every other Bluegrass horse born to run. I hope Last Chance makes it. I'd like to see Lady Elsmere have a horse of hers win the Kentucky Derby before she dies."

Asa remarked, "She'd better hurry."

"That's not funny."

"Wasn't meant to be."

We sat in silence again. Asa was correct that Lady Elsmere had very little time left, but I didn't want to think about it.

Asa spoke, "Mom, you'll never guess what this motel's name is."

"Surprise me."

"It's called the Last Chance Motel."

"You're kidding me?"

Asa shook her head. "Nope. I think you'll like it. It's a place where new chances are given. I can't explain it, but the motel is magical."

"If new beginnings are made there, the owner

should change the name," I said, intrigued.

"Maybe the motel will give us a new beginning. I know you're very angry with me, but I do what I have to do. Sometimes a cowboy in a white hat is not sufficient for what needs to be done. Sometimes it takes a dark knight with proficiency for violence. Know what I mean?"

"Asa, I don't want to talk about guns, spies, murder, or even the prospect of death. I want margaritas, sea breezes, manatees, and lots of seafood. Happy. That's what I want. Can we be happy for a week? Can we concentrate on that for a change?"

"May I say this?"

"What?" I snapped.

"I love you, Mom."

And that declaration, my friends, made everything right with the world. See you around the next spin of the planet.

Signing off.

Josiah Reynolds

You're not finished.
Keep going for the next Josiah Reynolds Mystery plus a *Prequel to Death By Theft* in an Asa short story—*Asa is Back!*

Josiah is looking forward to the county fair coming up soon. She comes across a battered tin box with a bunch of yellowed 3x5 note cards with her mother's old recipes. Nobody could make apple walnut cake like her mother. By golly, Josiah decides to make her mother's cake and enter it in this year's fair. It's sure to be a winner.

She makes a sample, asking Hunter and his new farm assistant, Palley, to try a slice. When the farm helper hears it's for the fair, the young man tells Josiah about the demolition derby each year. Ever since Palley received his driver's license, he has been waiting to be old enough to compete in the derby. The only problem is he needs an old car to enter.

Josiah tells Palley he is welcome to use an old jalopy that's been gathering dust in an unused shed on her property. Everyone's excited about going to the fair to see if the old beater car comes out a winner—until the trunk pops open to reveal—you guessed it—a body.

Whose body is it? How did it get there? Josiah is on the trail of murder again.

Keep going for the *Prequel to Death By Theft—*
ASA IS BACK!

Josiah Reynolds' daughter, Asa, spent her adult years striving to make the world a better place. However her chosen life has exacted its toll. Asa is broken in body and spirit.

Suffering an injury, Asa Reynolds flees to Key Largo to heal and reassess her life. Asa is depressed and feels she has made foolish mistakes in the past that have cost her much happiness. Still, Asa can't stop being Asa. She sees a little girl in need of help and decides to intercede the way only she can. And best part of all, Asa might have made a friend with Eva Hanover, owner of the Last Chance Motel. Eva tells Asa that the motel is magical and miracles happen. While Asa doesn't believe Eva's stories, she would welcome any help—even if it comes from mermaids and manatees.

Other Books By Abigail Keam

Josiah Reynolds Mysteries

Mona Moon Mysteries

Last Chance For Love Series

About The Author

Hi, I'm Abigail Keam. I write the award-winning *Josiah Reynolds Mystery Series* and the *1930s Mona Moon Mystery Series*. In addition, I write *The Princess Maura Tales* (Epic Fantasy) and the *Last Chance For Love Series* (Sweet Romance).

I am a professional beekeeper and have won awards for my honey from the Kentucky State Fair. I live in a metal house with my husband and various critters on a cliff overlooking the Kentucky River. I would love to hear from you, so please contact me. Until we meet again, dear friend, happy reading!

You can purchase books directly from my website:

www.abigailkeam.com

Made in the USA
Columbia, SC
01 November 2023